RENEGADE GUNS

Sam Kelly, meat contractor, watched the renegade Indians at their grim work and went in search of Ralph and Ernie, his friends and employees, intending to get the hell out. But he discovered that the renegades had found them first. Then, a knife in the back told Kelly that the redmen wanted his life too. However, he survived by a whisker — and he trod a path of death until he found a final shoot-out where he least expected it.

Books by Sam Gort
in the Linford Western Library:

GUNN CAME BACK

SAM GORT

RENEGADE GUNS

Complete and Unabridged

LINFORD
Leicester

First published in Great Britain in 1992 by
Robert Hale Limited
London

First Linford Edition
published 1996
by arrangement with
Robert Hale Limited
London

British Library CIP Data

Gort, Sam
    Renegade guns.—Large print ed.—
Linford western library
1. English fiction—20th century
2. Large type books
I. Title
823.9'14 [F]

ISBN 0–7089–7948–3

Published by
F. A. Thorpe (Publishing) Ltd.
Anstey, Leicestershire

Set by Words & Graphics Ltd.
Anstey, Leicestershire
Printed and bound in Great Britain by
T. J. Press (Padstow) Ltd., Padstow, Cornwall

This book is printed on acid-free paper

1

SAM KELLY peeped over the rock-pile at the edge of the ridge. He had been sure that a noise of some kind had echoed up to him from the floor of the valley below. Now he saw what had caused the sound. An Indian had shinned up a telegraph pole down there and was chopping away the lines and their insulators. Four other braves, all mounted, were watching the savage. The men, muscular and heavily bronzed, were wearing warpaint and down to breech-clouts and moccasins. They wore the eagle feathers of battle-tested dog soldiers in their hair, but it was noticeable that those astride were sitting their horses in the relaxed fashion of riders used to tooled saddles rather than the bare backs of prairie mustangs.

Renegades, Kelly decided. He was

looking at a handful of rebellious young bucks off one of the local reservations. Doubtless those red devils were bent on raiding where possible and killing palefaces whenever they got the chance. The varmints would never learn! These escapades invariably ended in the hanging of their perpetrators and the loss of privileges to the more peaceable of their brethren who had stayed at home. It couldn't be worth it. Yet, ten years after Red Cloud's visit to Washington and subsequent retirement to Wyoming's Agency lands, these outbreaks still occurred and there were plenty of whitemen about of the opinion that the Indian menace was not yet over and that a last big war would have to be fought to complete the submission of the Sioux.

Turning his head aside, Kelly spat. He had lived among the Indians at one time and had a certain amount of respect for them. He certainly didn't hate them, and preferred to regard what was happening here as none of his business. Yes, his chief consideration was for his scalp, but he did realize the disruption that the chopper below was going to cause among the white communities in this part of the world — and would not be against going out of his way to raise the alarm if he could do so without too much inconvenience to himself — but he had first to remember that he was a servant of the railroad and the possessor of a meat contract with the Union Pacific. His main consideration, regardless of everything else, must be to get his load of hump meat and venison — which his employees with the butcher's cart were bringing along somewhere to the south of here — over to head-of-steel, on the new cattleland's spur which was being built on this side of the Sweetwater River. Whatever else failed, the Company's tables must be kept filled for another fortnight. Let the Indians do their worst, he was determined to do only his best by the job that he had taken on.

He decided that it was time to get out of here, and started backing down to where he had left his horse. It seemed that scouting in this direction for buffalo had not been a good idea. But when could a man ever be certain that he was making the right move? He just hoped to goodness that those red miscreants would stay over this way and not come riding south. He and his two helpers, Ernie Crowe and Ralph Enders, were vulnerable enough at the best of times, but the meat waggon made them more so than ever. Just getting the load home was tough enough; he could do without fighting renegade Indians.

Reaching his horse, Kelly mounted up. He was far from happy about what he was doing, yet believed that he was acting for the best, since he didn't know the neighbourhood and had no idea of where a warning about what he had seen might have been delivered. The too zealous often did everybody a disservice anyway, so best get the hell and quiet his conscience with that undeniable sop.

He spurred his mount down the back of the ridge, then steered it through bands of thorn and pine scrub as he approached the foot of the downgrade. Now he passed into a small valley — which he had travelled earlier to reach this district — and followed it westwards, entering a tract of forest that was also familiar to him from his recent journeying. Angling his path to bisect the timber at its south-eastern corner, Kelly tried to judge the likely position of his butchers and the meat waggon on the prairie beyond the woods, but he knew that his riding had to be governed by approximates and didn't let his calculations tax him more than necessary. Ralph and Ernie couldn't be that far away, and he would come upon them in due course.

Reckoning the possibility of any immediate danger gone for now, Kelly relaxed a little and tried to enjoy his trot through the shadows of the woodland.

He was conscious of a real warmth in the May sunlight above the timbertops, and of new life stirring to the urges of the spring. There was young leaf everywhere, tender and pale green, and the breathing hush of the fronds below reached up into the boughs overhead and trapped the flutter of wings and piping of birdsong at its edges. The breeze stirred now and then, fresh with the memory of melted snows, and the heady odours of resin and sap came filtering down the aisles between the Douglas firs. It was all incredibly beautiful and indescribably joyous — and Kelly became forgetful and filled with the wonder of being alive — so that the sudden chill which settled over his mind did all the greater damage among his senses and he was possessed by an odd feeling of desperation. The need to find and rejoin Ralph and Ernie suddenly seemed more urgent than ever before. There was something wrong — or was it all imagination? Seeing those Indians had started it!

Kelly kicked for increased pace. Head bowed, he cleared the dragging foliage of the last timber. Ahead of him now coarse grass extended for as far as the eye could see and, far, far away to the south of him, a dim line of snowcaps placed the Park Range and the iridescent world of Colorado's rocky wonders. A moose boomed, and the echoes rolled for miles in the crystalline atmosphere. Kelly's spine magnetized and his nape bristled. He was again at one with the land — and yet that spoiling influence remained. He could feel human eyes upon him. There was no doubt about it: he was being watched! Rising in his stirrups, he looked slowly all around him. Nothing! Yet his instinct went on warning him that somebody was there. And he believed that whoever it was had been riding parallel with him even before he left the woods. It was not impossible that he had been spotted back there on the ridge and shadowed ever since. Or was he after

7

all too sensitive for his own good? If a man of the plains could ever be that!

Settling back into his saddle, Kelly eased both the revolver on his hip and the Winchester in his saddleboot. He rode onwards, full of uneasiness, yet also concentrating on the lie of the land and hoping that he would soon cut the waggon trace which would provide some indication of where Enders and Crowe might presently be found. The minutes went by. Nothing appeared on the ground ahead. Kelly's patience began to fray. He felt it to be time that points of reference were established, and first let his gaze move westwards. His eyes fixed on a hillock about five miles away. Ralph and Ernie, hampered by the meat vehicle, could hardly have travelled further than that since the dawn hour this morning, but it was no good galloping off in that direction before he made sure that the pair had got as far as this. So he looked the opposite way, trying to establish the day's starting point — and was not making a very good job of it, when movement caught his eye about two miles away and due east of him. Buzzards? Their circling presence just above the land was always disquieting when folk or animals were lost, but the fact they were flying there didn't have to mean a lot just now. Enders and Crowe might well have skinned out a buffalo back yonder and left the guts and less edible parts of the brute lying, as was the habit with all meat contractors; but the sign in the sky was nevertheless one which Kelly could not ignore, and he drew his horse round and headed for the wheeling birds.

The shadows of the vultures marked the spot, and Kelly arrived soon at the edge of a saucer-shaped depression. The hollow had a waterhole at its centre, and this was ringed by clumps of red willow and dogwood, with trampled breaks in the growth through which the creatures of the prairie obviously stepped up to drink. With his horse slowed to a walk, Kelly moved down into the circle of depressed earth — feeling now that there was something here to justify his apprehension — and it was a sprawling portion of the vegetation that briefly hid from him what he most feared to see, but it seemed that all at once the shape of the meat waggon was before him and beside it the body of a man.

Halting his horse, Kelly sprang to the ground. He ran to where the body lay, and turned it off its face, knowing already that he had found Ralph Enders. His employee and friend had been shot through the heart and must have died more or less instantly. Shocked all through, Kelly straightened up, forcing himself to think about what he had found — but his thoughts wouldn't hold firm — and a moment or two later he found himself walking a demented circle which passed through some reeds. Here he found Ernie Crowe grinning skywards. Ernie, too, had been shot through the chest and must have died within moments.

Kelly tipped back his head and looked at the sky, fighting to control his emotions. Murder had clearly been done at this spot. Ralph and Ernie had obviously been shot down in the coldest and most calculated of manners, probably from ambush. Kelly had the impression that the killing had been done when, on arriving here, the two men had turned aside to empty their bladders. It figured that the pair had intended to let the horse pulling the meat waggon drink at the nearby waterhole, and it was possible that the poor brute was still thirsty, but Kelly was frankly not interested in its needs just then and could only stand and seethe over what had occurred. It seemed a fair bet that those renegade Indians were responsible for this. They must have come upon the meat waggon and the two butchers while riding up from the Laramie direction. That would have been before they set about wrecking the telegraph line north of here. With the meat hunters unsuspecting, this depression had amounted to the perfect setting for murder.

Shutting his eyes, Kelly stood erect and breathed deeply for a few moments. Then, vaguely conscious that there was something here not quite as it should be, he opened his eyes again and studied Ernie Crowe's corpse anew. That done, he returned to Enders' body and considered that also in the light of his experience. His friends still had their scalps and had not been robbed. Now neither of those things fitted in with the crime that he had imagined. Renegade Indians left the reservations to rob and, like all their race, they prized scalps before anything. Was it possible that Crowe and Enders had not been killed by the renegade redmen after all? Yes, it was possible. But who else could have done this thing?

There was no ready answer to that. On the other hand, speculation could take a guy down paths without end. The certainty had gone out of everything.

There was now an element of mystery here, and curiosity as much as anything else sent Kelly walking in the direction of the spot from which he believed the killing shots had been fired and any possible clues that the murderers might have left behind.

A tiny Arctic tern went fluttering out of the dogwood at the waterhole's eastern end. The plodding Kelly took as little notice of its movement as he did the more violent departure of a blue jay from the willows at the opposite end of the water. Convinced that he was alone down here, Kelly paid no attention to these warning signs, and it came as a complete surprise to him when a hand suddenly clamped over his mouth from behind and he felt the point of a knife pierce his clothing and start entering his back.

Far stronger than most men — and inspired by an abrupt fear of death — Kelly wrenched his head round, breaking the hold which the hand had on his mouth. Now, at the corner of his gaze, he glimpsed a pudgy, cruel-eyed face, feather-topped and streaked with ochre, pressing up against his left shoulder, and he was about to strike backwards with his elbow on that side, when the knife really began to sink through the highly resistant muscle tissue of his middle back and create an intense and paralysing agony. His body went rigid, but for a moment his senses were amazingly heightened, and he seemed to smell, not the bear grease and hide of the average redskin, but the floury sweetness of short biscuits and the harsh odour of shag tobacco. Then the point of the knife, forced home remorselessly, reached his vitals and there was a red flash behind his eyes. The shapes about him turned into black silhouettes. They wavered briefly, then Kelly's knees buckled and he sank into oblivion.

He was a long while in the dark. Then the consciousness began to creep back into him. Now his mind suffered its own cold dawn. He had read an account once, in a paper from back East, of a man who claimed to have awakened on Jordan's bank just before being summoned back to earth from his expected trip into the Afterlife. Kelly wondered whether he was another such favoured being. But, as he raised his head — supposing that all things should be transfigured — he saw that nothing had changed in his vicinity. Everything appeared grey and dim and ordinary, and the stink of rank weeds and bad water seemed to be poisoning him. Agony permeated his frame, and his nerves dulled in a succeeding weakness. None of this was in line with what he had read of death and transfiguration. The Pastures of the Blessed were quite other than he had expected them to be. Or was it that he had arrived in the Hot Place? Perhaps his visions were those of hell upon earth.

No, it couldn't be that either. He could neither smell brimstone nor hear souls wailing in torment. And he didn't believe the denizens of hell kept horses either. Why horses? Well, there was one snorting very close to his head, and it sounded like his own. True, he thought ironically, any mount associated with him would be almost certain to land up Down Below, but this critter was behaving in such a normal manner that he could not believe it had died. So, by the parallel of this reasoning, it seemed unlikely that he had expired either, and most probable that the Indian's knife had somehow stabbed him through without quite managing to make a job of it.

He tried to get up. The horse sidled closer. Kelly lifted a hand and groped with the instinct of the blind. Fingers meeting a stirrup-iron, he clung on, and the horse walked forward. It dragged him clear of the bad smells, up a bumpy incline, over a stony brink, and out to a level place where the grass was thick and he could let go of the stirrup-iron again and lie flat on his stomach once more, aware now of the sunlight upon his back and a fearful thirst. "Thank you, old partner!" he muttered feebly. "Do the same for you come Michaelmas Day!"

The horse snorted contemptuously, and Kelly grinned against the earth. It had been brave talk all right. Small wonder the horse wanted no truck with it. Man or beast, who'd want another day like this anyway? His tongue seemed to stick to the roof of his mouth. He must have water; a drink was absolutely vital to him. There was a canteen on his saddle, and it should be full of liquid from a mountain spring. If only he could reach his pommel. Surely he was capable of that?

With eyes fast shut and mouth firmly crimped against the pain, Kelly forced himself up and backwards until he was kneeling on the grass. But the effort had been too much. There was no more strength in him; he was finished. Then he felt his mount's nose nudging and lifting at his chest. It was a sort of encouragement and, responding to a slight renewal within himself, he placed his hands on either side of the brute's headstall and hung on tightly, forcing his legs to straighten as the horse backed off with its head lifting. Suddenly he was erect, if still dependent on the animal's neck for ninety per cent of his support, and he reached down the mount's side and located his waterbottle, working it off the saddlehorn with difficulty and then contriving to draw its cork with his teeth.

Spitting out the stopper, Kelly put the canteen to his lips and drank greedily. The feel of it was good, and pints of water went down. Inevitably, he spewed up a large part of the liquid; but, once that suffering was over, he felt a great deal better and able to stand alone — capable, too, of opening his eyes and keeping them open. This time he thanked his horse in a humble voice. He had known before that the creature possessed understanding, but not in what degree, and his opinion of horseflesh generally had just been elevated a thousandfold. It made him realize that the old-timers had been right in describing the value of a good horse upon the prairie as 'beyond price.'

Kelly dropped his waterbottle. He simply hadn't the strength to return it to his pommel. Before all else, he must mount up, and he knew that would require every ounce of power and concentration that he possessed. He made his try — and it was indeed difficult enough — but he got there, and sat more or less erect in his saddle and looked down into the hollow adjacent, where the light from the westering sun fell upon his meat waggon and the bodies of Ralph Enders and Ernie Crowe.

It occurred to Kelly that there were things down there he ought to do — like covering the corpses against the buzzards and guiding the horse between the waggon's shafts down to the water's edge — but he knew that if he dismounted now he would never manage to get on to his horse a second time, so he would just have to hope that somebody else would come along soon and do what he couldn't do. He could see an enormous bloodstain at the spot where he had been lying, and it amazed him that he was still alive. No wonder he had needed all that water, for the pressure in his veins must be very low. It would be unwise to tempt Fate with any heroics. His number could still be up. He was bleeding heavily again, and the seat of his trousers was already tacky. He needed help, and must find it fast. If somebody didn't bind up that wound in his back before long, he would bleed down to his last pint and snuff it during the night. Next time he awakened, it might indeed be in the Hot Place.

He turned his horse northwards and set it in motion. Visions dim and vague crossed his imagination. He had this idea that, if he found the trail beside which that telegraph line ran — then followed it east or west — he must arrive in a township presently, or at least come upon somebody who would lend him a hand. He no longer had much fear of those renegade redmen — if that's what in fact they were — since he figured that they and his would-be killer would have completed their grim business in this district by now and got the hell out. If it wasn't like that — well, he'd just have to take his chance! Should that damned Indian with the knife want a second stab at him, he'd be happy to clip the fellow's ticket to the Happy Hunting Grounds with a slug from his Colt forty-four.

Kelly travelled slowly, and the scene around him grew misty again after that. He tried to keep his mind on what he was doing, but grew increasingly distrait. He used what little strength he had just to stay on his horse, and nothing seemed to matter very much any more. Presently the prairie, a faded place in the evening light, vanished about him, and he realized that he was back in the woods again. The glow above, endlessly broken by the timbertops, was confused and without shape or form, and Kelly found his mind further muddling amidst its hypnotic presence. He blinked repeatedly, for his eyes were giving out as his renewal of strength became smaller and smaller, and all at once he knew he could not ride any further. It had been a good try on his part, but now it was almost over. A man had only so much in him to use, and he had used it all. Quite soon now he was going to die, and the forest would have him. He was going, going — gone.

Then, as he toppled to the ground, he thought he heard a woman's voice. But that could not have been.

2

KELLY found himself lying in a featherbed when he came round again. He was warm, comfortable, and out of pain, and not feeling half as bad as he had when he had recovered consciousness out there on the plain. Weak he unquestionably was, and no doubt still tending to leak from the wound in his back, but he could feel that his hurt had been tightly bound up by hands that knew their business and that all danger of his bleeding to death had been averted. Nor did he have any suspicion this time that he had entered the Hereafter, for the scene in the lamplight about his newly opened eyes was as homely and familiar as any could be, and the old man and young woman who stood looking down upon him in their buckskin suits were obviously of the quick and American folk through and through. "Hello," he muttered. "What's the time?"

"Hello," the girl responded, the smile hovering about her clear blue eyes and pursed mouth a pleasant one. She gave her head a little toss, fanning her golden hair — which she had just freed from a tie of some kind — upon her square shoulders, and then she clasped her long-fingered, strong-looking hands beneath her breastbone and added: "You don't care what time it is."

"I do too," he informed her huskily.

"It's almost midnight," the girl said. "We brought you home from the forest, and Doctor McCarthy has been here to treat you. All right?"

"Near enough."

"You're to lie at rest and keep quiet."

"Am I?"

"The doctor said so."

"Bully for him!" Kelly applauded.

"He's the man," the old fellow observed pointedly, as grave and leathery

24

in the jib as his youthful companion was fresh and cheerful. He stroked at his thin white beard and made the air hiss in his small round nostrils. "Why don't you give yourself a chance, son? You've been badly hurt."

"I know it," Kelly assured him. "And I'm grateful to both of you for your help. I thought I heard a woman's voice as I fell off my horse."

"That was me," the girl acknowledged.

"You?"

"Jean Troy."

"I'm Pete Troy," the old man added. "This girl's grandpa. She's my late son's daughter."

"You're good people."

"Shucks!" Pete Troy responded. "Couldn't leave you out there to die. Wouldn't have left a dog to do that."

"When you fell off your horse," the girl explained, "we put you right back on — bent over the saddle — and brought you here. We'd been setting our traps. You were lucky, Mr — We

25

don't often go out into the woods as far as we did today."

"The name's Kelly — Sam Kelly. I guess I've been altogether lucky. I ought to be dead. That knife must have just missed every organ in my body that mattered."

"McCarthy said so," Pete Troy confirmed. "Who did it to you?"

"Looked like an Indian," Kelly answered. "I caught just a glimpse of him as the blade was piercing me. A buck in warpaint — off the Laramie reservation most like. Damned renegade!"

"G'damned Sioux!" the old man seethed. "The only good one ever was a dead one!"

"Don't you dare spit in here, Grandfather!" the girl admonished, a finger lifted.

"Wasn't going to," Pete Troy lied, swallowing his spittle. "They killed your father, girl."

"Yes, I know."

"We feed 'em, Kelly," the old man

snarled. "We clothe 'em, we house 'em, we even put dollars in their wampum bags — and what do we get? We get raids here, burning there, and murder all over! You can't be kind to an Indian, 'cos the skunk don't understand what kindness is. Kindness to him is a cut throat!"

"This land was lately their land," the girl reminded, "and they were free to roam as they wished. They're brutal savages — and I'm afraid of them — but we have to be fair."

"Aw, stuff and nonsense!" Troy growled. "You can't be fair to a redskin. He just sticks a knife into a whiteman's back. That's his fairness. All you can do is watch out when the hellion's around — and get him before he gets you!"

"I sure didn't watch out," Kelly muttered weakly. "I turned my back when I shouldn't have. Yet it wasn't that I hadn't a warning of sorts. The fact is, I'd seen a small bunch of redmen cutting down the telegraph wires where they run through a valley that can't be far from here. But I had business elsewhere and sheared off."

"What business, Kelly?"

"I had to get back to my meat waggon," Kelly returned. "I did that, and found that my butcher pals had been gunned down beside a waterhole that has dogwood and red willows about it. Not scalped either. Hardly the Sioux style, eh?"

"You're a meat contractor?" the old man hazarded.

"You have me pegged," Kelly acknowledged. "I've got a contract with the Union Pacific. I expect you know they're putting in a spur for the cattlemen up near the Sweetwater. It's my job to keep the tracklayers in fresh meat."

"Yep, I've heard about that spur," Troy said. "If you saw them redskins chopping down the telegraph line, son, shouldn't you have raised the alarm? From what I know, you weren't a mile from Clattville — that's the town below where our cabin stands — and the folk there didn't know about that war party till long past too late. I mean — well, they took out after them red sidewinders after the Sioux had played a modest hell and rode on. Which left the town wide open to what happened next, d'you see?"

"Next?"

"Guess you'd call it a coincidence."

"Coincidence?"

"We heard it from Doctor McCarthy," the girl cut in, while bending over the bed to peer somewhat anxiously into the patient's face. "Are you feeling okay, Mr Kelly?"

"Sure. Don't I look it?"

"No," Jean Troy said self-reproachfully. "We're supposed to be keeping you quiet, but here we are running on nineteen to the dozen."

"Oh, doctors!" Kelly sniffed contemptuously. "Bunco men! I'm fine. Tell me about that coincidence."

"While the townsmen were away, chasing the Indians, Clattville was

29

attacked by a gang of whitemen," the girl explained. "The whitemen cleaned out the bank, helped themselves from the emporium, and shot up the town generally." She shook her head, grimacing. "Everything comes at once, doesn't it? In life you always see it!"

"I guess you do," Kelly admitted.

"It sounds to me like you could've helped Clattville, mister," old Pete Troy reflected. "When didn't we have to put ourselves out to do the right? You happy with yourself?"

"He had his own business to attend to," the girl said reasonably. "Do we go hunting trouble, Grandpa?"

"I don't know these parts," Kelly said defensively. "I didn't know that Clattville was nearby. This isn't my part of the globe. Was from Kansas originally — via the Army and all sorts."

"Well, we can't hold it against you, I suppose," the ancient trapper said. "But I wouldn't make it a subject of talk outside, was I you?"

"I'm not plain crackers!" Kelly retorted. "I'm in mess enough for now." He pulled a face. "Can you believe in such a coincidence?"

Jean Troy and her grandfather nodded. They seemed to have no suspicions about what had occurred. Indeed, it could well be that there was no cause for any. But Kelly remembered the inconsistencies of his day all too well. Not least the smells of short biscuit and shag tobacco on the Indian who had stabbed him. There had likewise been the manner in which those renegades had sat their horses. Small things, yes, but they seemed to point to something novel in the way of crime. Yet if he had his suspicions, he didn't want to stir up a hornet's nest for himself. All he wanted now was to get well as quickly as he could and return to his own affairs. When everything else was stripped away, he was a poor man with his living to earn, and he couldn't spare the time to worry about rights and wrongs. The world and its tragedies had always been there, and he was content to let those who could afford it fight the dragons. "I reckon I am tired at that," he said faintly.

"We can talk again tomorrow," Jean Troy said. "If you're up to it."

"I'll be up to it," Kelly promised, licking his lips. "I sure am thirsty."

"Get him a cup of water, girl," Pete Troy ordered. "You can make him some broth for later."

Jean nodded. Kelly watched her turn away from the bed and walk into the next room, where he heard movements that suggested she was filling a cup from a bucket of water. He felt the old trapper's eyes upon him as he awaited the girl's return. Kelly realized that, despite his expressions to the contrary, Troy had no very good opinion of him — and that shamed and irritated him some — but the trapper said nothing further. He waited for the return of his granddaughter, saw Kelly given a drink, and then went out, leaving Jean to attend to a few little niceties around the bed and wish Kelly 'goodnight'.

The patient muttered a rejoinder, then closed his eyes as a shadow settled over his consciousness; and almost at once he was back in that dark place where he had spent so much time just lately. Few dreams came — and none that mattered — and when he awakened again the night had flown, the lamp was out, and the room was full of sunlight.

There was still a lot of pain in his back, but he eased himself into a sitting position against his pillow and assessed himself as much stronger and mending from his wound. He was hungry too, and looking forward to some of that broth which Pete Troy had spoken of last night. Blinking around him, he saw that he had the room to himself, and he lifted the bedclothes and discovered that he was naked save for his long pants and the thick bandages which encircled his midriff. Listening now, he heard nobody about and, aware of how quickly a man lost his mobility through lying about, he got out of bed and forced himself to stand erect. Faintness threatened him at once, and he staggered to the window opposite his bed and hung on to the sill, looking out dizzily on a scene of truly remarkable beauty.

His head began to clear and, though he still felt weak, he knew that he had full control of himself again. He peered more closely at the rugged slope beyond the window which fell towards the rooftops of the small town that stood compactly in the valley below. He could make out reefs and stone-piles on the downgrade that were covered with ivy and other creepers, and there were trees present too, waves and clusters of them, but so placed that they enhanced rather than obscured the prospect as a whole, and Kelly judged that the cabin in which he was standing predated the town below and had probably been built when the valley floor was a part of the wilderness and alive with game. For water, the first need of all life, threaded the growth which still choked the back of the low place, and there were signs that the stream was still visited by the larger animals of the nearby forest which had learned to tolerate the nearby town.

About then he heard a woman's voice start singing. The sound came from the left and outside the cabin wall. Pressing his nose against the glass, he angled his gaze in the direction of the song, and a washing ground became visible to his eye. There he saw Jean Troy. Divested of her hunting attire now, she was clad in a skirt and check shirt, and he perceived that she had perhaps the best figure that he had ever seen on a woman. Despite his greatly weakened state, he desired her, and he wondered whether his need would find any response in her; but he deemed her a superior woman in every way and knew that he would always behave himself around her. Nature had designed her for a better man than Samuel Kelly. It hurt him to admit it, of course, but a guy had to face facts. He was both poor and afflicted with a fiddlefoot. No catch for a good girl.

Kelly gave a start and glanced round as the bedroom door opened. Pete Troy sauntered in, hands in pockets and shoulders hunched. "Morning," he greeted.

"Morning," Kelly responded.

"Taking a bit of a chance, wouldn't you say?"

"How so?"

"Dressed like that. It's only May."

"I'm warm enough," Kelly lied.

"Well, there."

"Mr Troy," Kelly said thoughtfully, "I'd like to ask a favour of you."

"What?"

"I told you yesterday about those friends of mine lying dead on the prairie."

"It's taken care of, Sam," the trapper said. "You told us enough to go by. Jean went down into Clattville at sunup. She told the sheriff what had happened to you and your pals over yonder. A party's gone out to the waterhole to bring your waggon and the bodies in." He scratched his chin through the white hair of his beard. "Did right, didn't we?"

"Why, sure," Kelly replied heartily, as if there had been no need to ask — yet not adding that he would have been happier had the trapper and his granddaughter kept the law out of it, for you could never be sure how far a sheriff's inquiries would go, and he hadn't been blameless in this matter. "I'll pay you for your trouble when I get a few dollars in my pocket."

"Forget it, son," Troy advised shortly. "You're maybe too independent for your own good. It ain't often Jean and me get the chance to help somebody. Her grandma, my late missus, was the helpin' kind, and there never was a kindness she did we had any cause to regret."

"Then I hope you'll have no cause to regret this one."

"Trust and obey," Troy observed.

37

"Ain't that what the Good Book commands us to do?"

"Um," Kelly grunted non-committally, for he had never been quite sold on the Good Book and blind faith.

Then Jean Troy walked into the bedroom. "What on earth are you doing out of bed?" she demanded angrily. "You shouldn't be standing around like that. You'll catch your death of cold!"

"Unlikely," Kelly said. "I've years of roughing it behind me, and I've known what it is to be really cold. Forty below for days on end."

"You're bleeding again!"

"Now I am sorry about that," he said, sincerely contrite. "Put down some old piece to save your sheets."

Looking fierce, the girl clapped her hands. "Get back into bed this instant! Doctor McCarthy would be furious if he could see you now!"

"The sheets — "

"Confound the sheets!"

Kelly returned to bed very meekly

38

indeed. He even allowed himself to be bundled from this side to that as he was tucked in.

"A handful of salt will usually take bloodstains out of cotton," Pete Troy reminded, grinning at the younger man's discomfiture. "Didn't expect that, did you? Her mama was a pretty girl too — but she could fly!"

"Sorry," Kelly mumbled.

"If you want us to help you," the girl informed him, "you must do what's necessary to help yourself."

"All right, Jean," her grandfather said rather sternly, "that's enough. Don't nag the boy. Fair miracle he can stand like that. Feed him."

"Right away," Jean said, a twinkle in her eye. "Just so long as he knows who's boss."

"Never had any doubt," Kelly assured her, lifting his hands in surrender.

"Now he's taking the Irish out of me," the girl said, shaking her head at her grandfather.

"Not true!" Kelly protested.

"It hadn't better be," she said, tossing her head as she made for the door.

"Jean!" her grandfather called.

Checking, she looked across her shoulder. "Yes?"

"Any word up from town yet about this fellow's waggon and such?"

"No, Grandfather," she replied. "I'll go down into Clattville again later on and ask what's happened. The sheriff is unlikely to send anybody up." She glanced at the man lying on the bed. "It isn't that important, is it?"

"It isn't important at all," Kelly assured her. "Forget about it for now. Thank you for your trouble."

Jean Troy nodded and resumed her retreat, while her grandfather went to the window and looked out, pulling an ear. "That question of mine sounded damn silly, didn't it? Fact is, I thought I saw somebody coming up the path from town a while ago. I must have been mistaken." He yawned audibly. "Oh-ha. Not for the first time. Reckon I'll go out and sit on the verandah — have

40

a nod. That's mostly what I'm best at these days. The traps can wait an hour anyhow." Then he, too, vacated the room.

Left to himself once more, Kelly lay with nostrils twitching at the smell of beef broth which was wafting to him from the further end of the log-house. He thought his own thoughts until Jean Troy re-entered carrying a tin tray on which a basin of broth was perched. At a word from the girl, he raised himself and allowed her to feed him with a spoon — which she did very skilfully — then, when he had emptied the basin and she showed no disposition to stay and talk, he sank back onto his pillow and shut his eyes again, drifting into a sleep which seemed full of childhood and that endless labour on his father's farm.

There had, too, been all that talk of the Civil War that was then being fought back East. Union sympathizers, he and his family had never expected to be touched by the conflict so far away. But then Bill Quantrill and his raiders had swept through the district one day and Kelly had found himself fatherless and elevated to the status of manhood at twelve years old. He had done his best, toiling in the fields with Ma until they were both fit to drop, and all had gone along somehow until his remaining parent had taken mortal sick and he had been forced to do the little he could for her until she had died when he was fifteen.

After that, tossed off the farm because he could no longer pay the rent, he had given up the land and worked as he could. He had been a teamster, cowboy, miner, section hand and lumberjack — all before he was twenty. And since then he had done the same things over again, ending up as a meat contractor and now a wounded man lying in somebody else's bed. It had surely been a poor turn out so far, and he couldn't see it getting any better. Indeed, as he grew older and his strength decreased, it would most likely get worse. Yet the one inferior thing to being alive without hope was to be dead and buried. At least he was still alive and functional, and that was a heck of a lot more than could be said for Ralph Enders and Ernie Crowe. It was time to count his blessings.

He opened his eyes, determined to get right inside that wound of his and heal it by tomorrow night. It was all a matter of visualizing what he wanted. Concentrate. But then his mind was thrown out of kilter as he heard a slight bump from the exterior of the wall on his right and a faint brushing noise along the timbers after that. Now he listened tensely, eyes fixing on the window opposite his bed, for he knew there was somebody creeping along the wall out there and expected them to show themselves at any instant.

His heartbeat quickened and there was a sudden dryness in his mouth. Then a barely perceptible shadow spread across the window-glass and a presence edged in behind it, the pitiless eyes in a fleshy face pressing up for a close look through the panes and focusing momentarily upon the bed beyond them and the man in it. For a split second the eyes betrayed a startled recognition — and then they were gone, and Kelly had the feeling that he had just suffered an optical illusion of a rather horrible kind.

Yet his common sense told him that he had indeed been looked in upon, and he left his bed again and staggered over to the window, ending up with his nose squashed painfully against the glass and his gaze slanting to the right. He saw nobody. The intruder had seemingly vanished from the open ground along the eastern side of the log-house. It went without saying, of course, that the man had already passed around the nearer southern angle of the cabin and was now fleeing at top speed onto ground beyond which Kelly had yet to see.

Well, he couldn't give chase; that one was out of the question. And it was already too late to call for Jean Troy or her grandfather. So he must trust his own senses entirely about the face that he had just glimpsed so briefly, and draw his own conclusions as to what its presence had meant. For of one thing he was certain. He had just looked again upon the face of the man who had knifed him out on the prairie.

3

KELLY made a shaky return to his bed. Watching the door as he got back between the sheets, he half expected Jean Troy to put her head in at any moment and begin upbraiding him again; but in fact the girl did not reappear and he covered himself once more and lay considering what had just occurred. That man — his would-be killer — was no Indian. Devoid of warpaint and his eagle feather, the guy had been all too plainly an overstuffed member of the white race — which no doubt accounted for why he had smelled of short biscuit and shag tobacco.

What was he to make of it? Only what he had suspected but refused to entirely credit a while ago. Those Indians whom he had seen busting up the telegraph line had not been Indians at all. They were whitemen dressed up as red and playing a part. Their game was obvious enough. While got up to resemble Sioux dog soldiers, they did open damage in and around settled places. This immediately brought the irate members of the white male population out to hunt them. Then either they reverted to their normal plains dress and colouring — or, more likely, a waiting band of white confederates — rode into the now undefended town or whatever and robbed and pillaged at will. It was a neat ruse, when you came to think about it, for the renegades could always elude their hunters by breaking up and resuming their white identities. As for the rest, it figured that the knifeman had returned to the waterhole on the prairie at some time after wounding Kelly, found the meat contractor's body and horse missing — probably to his considerable consternation — then come to Clattville this morning and perhaps overheard talk of the injured man brought in from the forest and now lying up in Pete Troy's cabin. The pattern was there all right and, give or take small differences in detail, almost certainly what had happened. Thus 'pudgy face' had seen him and knew that he was still alive — something that could hardly add to the Kelly peace of mind; for it went without saying that he could look for another attempt on his life before long; since, having just been spotted himself, the renegade would realize the risk that his enemy would put two and two together and guess that a kind of variation on the Texas Comanchero operation was taking place up here in Wyoming.

So what was to be done about it? Kelly wasn't sure. He had no real proof of this white two-facedness. What he had deduced was all in his own mind; there was no material evidence to go on. If he went to the law as soon as he could, it was not improbable that he would be treated with incredulity — since folk didn't usually wish to believe the worst about their own kind — and he had already seen that Pete Troy and Jean were ready to accept events as they had happened. No, regardless of the danger to himself — and in further recognition of the fact that he had not behaved as well towards Clattville as he might have done — he would do well to go on holding his noise and hope that other testimony would emerge at some future date. Trouble was, no matter how careful the watch he kept on himself, he might get finished off before he could pass on what he believed he knew to anybody who mattered. He just didn't know which way to turn in his dilemma; and, on top of a certain weakness that he could sense in his reasoning, there was always the unpredictability of the kind of human action coming along that would take the renegades into more distant parts and all memory of their doings at this place with them.

Kelly had to let it go at that, for just then Doctor McCarthy came in to visit him. The medico was a big, bluff, friendly man — a snuff user with the disposition to sit and chat about human foibles — and, detecting the underlying impatience of the Kansan's nature, he advised Kelly to relax and forget everything trying for a week or so. Nothing, he assured the younger man, was ever achieved by haste, and little was ever lost through honest delay. Yes, yes — he knew all about the Union Pacific Railroad and the stringency of their meat contracts; but the setback was already present, and a fully recovered man could much better make his apologies and pick up the pieces than one who was still unwell and tried to get back into harness too soon.

It was all very good advice, and Kelly, feeling more worn by the events of the day than the doctor could possibly know, felt constrained to take it; so, while lying with his gun under his pillow at all times, he let things take their course and the days drift by, with the result that a fortnight passed before Doctor McCarthy declared him healed and ceased making calls. But the doctor had to be paid — and the uncomplaining Pete Troy also deserved his recompense — so Kelly decided that he must reduce his single asset as soon as he could and pay what was owing. To that end, after he had eaten his dinner and retired to the verandah to take his ease — on the day of McCarthy's final visit — he called to Jean Troy, who was again seeing to the laundry on the washing ground to his left, and she looked up from her basket and asked what he wanted.

"Will you tell me something?" he responded.

"What do you want to know?"

"Come over here."

"You're a nuisance, Sam Kelly!"

"Always have been," he assured her good-naturedly.

The girl walked slowly towards him, drying damp hands on the front of her apron. "Well?"

"I need to sell my waggon and horse," he answered. "You told me the townsmen got them home in good shape. Who'd be most likely to buy them at a fair price?"

"In Clattville?" Jean queried.

He nodded, considering her patiently, since it had never crossed his mind to think of going further afield.

"Sam," she said bluntly, "I think it's more a question of who will give you any price. You might dicker with one or two of the farmers from outside town, but it's my opinion only Ben Burgess is likely to buy."

"Who's he, Jean?"

"Ben runs a general freight business in Clattville," she replied. "What were you hoping to get?"

"Three hundred and fifty dollars. For the waggon and the horse."

"I don't believe Ben would pay that."

"I'd take two-fifty — and be considerably the loser."

She smiled doubtfully. "Well, it's a better figure to start at."

"You'd tell me anything," he accused, chuckling.

"These aren't wealthy parts, Sam," the girl denied, a far-away look in her eyes. "A little money has to go a long way in Clattville. The more so after that raid. What's more, your circumstances are known, and I figure Ben Burgess will be reasoning much as I at this moment. You're in straits, Sam, and will take just about anything you can get."

"If only folk would play something like fair!" Kelly complained.

"When was business ever governed by fairness, Sam?"

"You have me there!" Kelly admitted. "I'll walk down into the town before long and look up this guy Burgess."

"No, Sam," Jean Troy advised. "Let me do your bargaining for you. I think I can get you a better deal than you'll ever make for yourself. I've known Ben since I was a little girl."

Kelly looked her up and down, a knowing grin at his mouth and eyes.

"Yeah, a pretty girl is always at an advantage among men. Okay — if it's not putting on you? Remember, you'll be bargaining for yourself too. Some of the money has to go to you and your grandpa. Entirely by right."

"We haven't helped you for what we can get out of it," the girl said shortly. But then she shrugged and gave a little nod. "You have to keep your pride, yes — and our trapline barely meets our needs. We're too near civilization to make good catches. A few years ago my grandfather was of the mind to make a new home out in the wilds, but I was against that. I've always preferred to live with folk and have the conveniences of a nearby town. I want to see more life, not less. I guess grandfather understands that. He's never pressed for a new cabin in the woods."

"I should think not," Kelly said, gazing towards the far timbertops for which Pete Troy had left at sunup. "You have your best years ahead of you, Jean, and he clearly had the best years of his life ages ago. You're the blessing of his old age, and he'd be a rare fool if he didn't know it. He can't afford to lose you. But I wonder where it'll leave you if he lives to be a hundred — or even ninety?"

Jean Troy lowered her face and frowned, obviously a trifle angered.

"None of my business!" he hastened. "Reckon I was thinking aloud. You've become a presence in my mind."

"Do you think I don't see it too?" the girl asked sharply. "But things are as they are, Sam. I'm doing no more than repay a debt to my grandparents for what they did in my upbringing."

"You can't be other than you are," Kelly assured her — "and I wouldn't have you so."

"It is none of your concern," Jean said far more gently. "Have you got the bill of sale from your waggon, Sam? Ben Burgess will naturally want to see it to be sure that the vehicle is yours to sell."

"I've got it," he said. "Indoors. It's in the wallet I keep my business papers in. You'll remember it. The one old Pete took off my horse, with my spare clothing and other items. Want me to go indoors and find it up?"

"Yes, please," she answered. "And I'll have that shirt of yours before you go. It's about ready to walk off by the look of it."

"You women and your cleanliness!" Kelly grumbled, removing his old leather jacket, dropping it on the bench beside him, then pulling off his shirt and tossing it to her. "Where's the harm wearing a shirt for a week? A mite of dirt never did me any harm yet!"

"Oh, Sam!" the girl chided gravely, holding up his frankly soiled shirt by its rumpled collar and studying it with an air of extreme distaste and disapproval. "What are we to do with you?"

Looking suitably shamefaced, Kelly cleared his throat and walked indoors, going through to the room which had been his ever since he had been carried into the log-house by Jean Troy and her grandfather. There he sought out his saddlebags, removed and put on another shirt, then located the wallet of which he had spoken and hunted for his waggon's bill of sale, finding it behind the meat contract which he had signed last fall with the Union Pacific Railroad.

Placing the bill of sale on his pillow, Kelly sat down on his bed and unfolded the contract, slowly going through its clauses with a distracted mind. He hoped there might be some advantage in the agreement which he had missed before, but there was nothing — as he had really known must be the case: it being specific that attack by hostiles was lumped in with the Acts of God — and he was finally compelled to accept, again as he had really known from the beginning, that his contract with the Union Pacific had simply given him a job and little more. All the penalty clauses left him heavily forfeit. If the U.P. liked to press it — which he guessed they would do if he gave them any trouble — he could actually end up paying in hard cash for whatever money the railroad had lost through buying fresh meat from another source due to the default of their contractor. It didn't look good, and Kelly felt that, if he hoped for any dealings with the Union Pacific in future years, he would do well to visit their office in South Hill, explain precisely what had happened to him, beg their pardon for any inconvenience caused, and promise his best efforts on their behalf if they ever gave him a chance in time to come. Doing what he proposed could work out to his disadvantage, of course, but it appeared to him the only honourable way of doing things just then.

Rising tiredly, Kelly packed away those objects which were to go away. After that he took the bill of sale off his pillow and started walking back towards the cabin and the washing ground where he supposed Jean Troy to be still at work, since he had not heard her re-enter the cabin during the time that he had been in his bedroom. Then, as he neared the threshold, he heard the report of a shot from not too far away outside, and he was frowning a slight puzzlement as to what the noise could mean, when he heard Jean Troy give vent to a sudden blood-chilling scream.

Dropping the piece of paper which he held, Kelly went bounding outside on to the verandah. He stopped abruptly as he became conscious of the girl standing beside a table on the drying ground to his left which supported a washtub. He watched her eyes, for he could not understand why she was staring aghast at the verandah seat that was situated on his right; and then, suddenly grasping that something was badly amiss in that direction, he turned his head sharply and saw that old Pete Troy — who must have come home in recent minutes and was now wearing the leather jacket of which Kelly had divested himself before pulling off his dirty shirt — was lying slouched upon the seat, his head and shoulders thrown back against the logs of the cabin wall and a bloodstain upon his chest. He had clearly been shot, and was just as obviously dead.

Throwing off his brief paralysis, Kelly went to the ancient woodsman and stood over him, uncertain of what to do, but he went staggering aside an instant later as Jean Troy came leaping onto the verandah and gave him a powerful shove. Then, having thus made space for herself, the girl dropped to her knees before the shot man and kept thrusting his drooping head erect — plainly in the hope that it would stiffen back into position and prove that life was still present — but each time old Pete's jaw levelled only to fall forward again, and Jean finally gave it up and rocked back on her knees. "Oh, no!" she wailed. "Grandfather — oh, no!"

Taking a deep breath, Kelly calmed himself in both mind and body. With the angle of Pete Troy's wound fixed in his eye, he faced eastwards and judged the line up which the bushwhacker's bullet had travelled, deeming that it had come from a clump of scrub fir and box elder at the edge of the Troy property and almost opposite the cabin's front door.

It had indeed been virtually the perfect position from which to trigger the fatal shot, and Kelly's instinct was to charge the rough mass of growth across the way — on the chance that the killer was still there to be flushed out — but he was fairly sure that the man would have withdrawn almost at once and that the other was probably a good distance from the clump now. Inbred to that, Kelly was forced to admit to himself that he was still not fit enough for a hard chase over a rugged hillside on which the fleeing rifleman would have every opportunity to turn on him and shoot again.

No, the risk there became the more foolish as Kelly fully perceived the grim fact that the bushwhacker had shot the wrong man and would be given another opportunity to get the right one if he set off in pursuit. Then he was stunned into immobility as Jean Troy, sounding like the voice of his, Kelly's own conscience, said bitterly: "That bullet was meant for you, Sam!"

"I've no doubt of it," Kelly admitted glumly.

"You've no doubt of it?" the girl queried, a note of shocked indignation now coming to her voice. "I can't credit you're telling me that you knew the killer was aware you were up here with us."

"I feared it," he confessed awkwardly, since he had no wish to defend himself with lies.

"Please explain."

"I saw somebody spying in at my window one day."

Amazement, both hurt and angry, showed on Jean's face. "You didn't tell us!"

"Mostly because I supposed myself the only person at risk," Kelly said helplessly. "I think there's a heck of a lot more to all this than you know. Nor did I ever dream anything like this could happen. We've obviously been watched and our habits noted. I've often worn that old leather jacket of mine just lately. What made your grandfather pick it up and put it on?"

"He got home sooner than he or I expected," Jean Troy replied. "As I did with you, I asked him for his shirt, thinking that I might as well wash it with everything else today, and he took his shirt off and put your coat on. It's cool in the shadows now."

"So, togged out like me, he sat down in his favourite spot," Kelly said solemnly. "How long had he been sitting there?"

"A quarter of an hour — perhaps a little more."

"If only I had come out sooner!"

"The right man would have got shot?"

"If that's how you want to word it."

"I don't, Sam!" she protested. "If you'd done this, if you'd done that, if you'd done something else. My grandmother would often remark on 'if' being a little word with a big meaning. How often can we be sure that we're doing the right thing? I prefer to think this was fated. I can see the pattern."

"So can I," Kelly said sourly, trying to keep a note of derisiveness out of his tones. "Except that I don't believe in fate or much else. It is up to us, Jean. We may not intend to do the wrong, but if we do, everything turns out wrong afterwards. I did the wrong thing — both this afternoon and when that renegade hellion looked in through my bedroom window."

"It might have altered something," the girl allowed. "How much have you been holding back, Sam?"

"Something," he confessed, throwing up his hands rather hopelessly. "What's

64

the good of frightening folk to death or rousing their scorn? I know you've cause to be angry with me."

"Yes, but I'm not going any further down that track, Sam," Jean Troy said firmly. "We've got too much trouble here to quarrel over who may have been to blame for what. Perhaps I drew the evil to this spot — with that thought of mine about how nice it would be to see a little more of life than I have seen so far. Well, that poor old man won't live to be a hundred — or even ninety — now."

"You didn't mean it like that," Kelly said indignantly, "and neither did I. We were talking, that's all."

"We were talking," the girl agreed. "Let's carry Grandfather indoors. It's my duty to do for him what has to be done."

"No," Kelly said, with just enough authority in his voice to make the girl hesitate. "The town isn't quarter of a mile away. There must be an undertaker down there, and a proper person to do the corpse washing and such. If we were way out yonder in the woods, it would be a different matter. Here we should be able to buy the services we need and get a proper burying done."

"I — I don't like failing him at the last," Jean Troy said, her voice faltering. "He — he did so much for me — "

"You won't be failing him," Kelly interrupted, carefully lowering the dead man from the seat to the boarding of the verandah floor, where he straightened Troy's limbs and then covered the lifeless face with a big red and white-spotted handkerchief taken from a trouser-pocket. "You can safely leave him there, Jean. Go indoors and have a cry, if that's what you need. I'm going to walk down into Clattville. I'll speak with the undertaker and the sheriff. I don't imagine it will be all that hard to locate either."

"Are you up to it, Sam?"

"I think so," he answered. "I don't

think I'm up to gallivanting all over the auction for a day or two more, but I reckon I can handle ordinary things."

"What will you tell the sheriff?"

"I don't know," Kelly returned unhappily. "I'll have to tell you after I've told him. I haven't the faintest notion what I'm going to say next. I don't know what the man will be prepared to believe."

"I don't think I follow you, Sam."

"I don't suppose you do," he sighed. "It has to do with renegade Indians who might in fact be white crooks. I've kept what I think about that in the dark because I haven't been altogether sure about the truth behind so much else." Kelly flinched off a smile. "I've never been a guy to shoot off his mouth overmuch. I guess I don't express myself so good."

"You do all right, mister!" the girl insisted.

"Just maybe," he said, stepping down from the verandah and moving away from her. "This errand won't run itself."

"Hurry back!" she urged.

Kelly raised a hand to show that he had heard her, but didn't look round again. Instead he lengthened his stride and passed around the southern end of the cabin, seeing a path that led down the rugged hillside before him towards the town. A very strange feeling came to him then, for he had gazed down upon the rooftops of Clattville so often — from the vantage of the Troy property — that he had come to regard the scene as a kind of picture hanging on the wall of his mind. Now he was about to enter that picture and there seemed to be a question in him as to whether he would become part of its stilly presence or go on belonging to the place of blood and tears above.

But the illusion and its question mark faded as Kelly, little sapped by walking steeply downhill, entered Clattville and found himself in just another flimsy Western town. Halting at the middle of the main street — which was the only street in all that mattered — Kelly looked first up the street and then down it, reading the signs that jutted above the boardwalks, and he located the funeral parlour just a few paces away to his right. The undertaker, one Silas Vance, turned out to be a funny little fellow, fat-bellied, small-footed, and fish-faced — not unlike some ageing gnome from a woodcut in a child's storybook — and he stood rheumy-eyed and round-mouthed while Kelly informed him of Pete Troy's murder and the need to arrange for the deceased's funeral. Somehow it all seemed just out of drawing — and appeared the more so when Silas Vance took down his top hat, with its mourning band of black silk, and placed it on top of his head, wearing it like a badge of office — then shouted for his assistant in a thin, piping voice and declared that Mr Kelly could leave it all to them. "Fine," his customer said. "Where do I find the sheriff?"

"The sheriff, sir? Matt Coggan, sir? Why, at the other end of the street, sir — on this side, sir."

Simple as that. But then 'sir' had known it must be, and he left the funeral parlour and walked eastwards for a hundred yards — to a point where the road began bending away from town and into distances unknown — and there found the law office and its incumbent, the large, flint-eyed Matt Coggan, a man of humourless presence and intimidating personality. Still bemused and strangely overhung, Kelly went blurting into an account, not only of Pete Troy's killing, but his own recent life, going through it detail by detail — from what he had witnessed of the telegraph line's destruction to the deceased's folly in putting on the leather jacket — but Coggan seemed to do little more than take it all with a pinch of salt and finally said: "It makes a fine yarn, Mr Kelly, but so does last Christmas. What the deuce am I supposed to do

70

about it this far on? That attack on Clatville is booked to an unknown gang, and the trouble we had with the Indians on the same day was just more Indian trouble. It's all part of the time, and a lawman learns better than to go seeking complications — for there usually are none. Crooks, as a class, aren't that bright, you know." He glowered out of the window, watching a black-clad old biddy emerging from the general store. "As for Pete Troy, I'm sorry he's dead, of course, and I'll investigate his killing as thoroughly as I can — all as a matter of my sworn duty — but I doubt I'll get anywhere with it. There's your malarkey about some renegade chief — which certainly adds a note of mystery, as they say — but I wouldn't mind betting that Pete died at the hands of some trapper settling an old score. He could be a contrary cuss, and I've heard rumours that he wasn't above robbing another man's traps. What would you say to that?"

"Hell!"

"But nought to do with you and the curious tale you've been spinning, eh?"

"No," Kelly responded almost fiercely, and went to point out the strengths of his case; but he soon perceived that he was beating a dead horse, for the sheriff was plainly a rigid man who had made up his mind not to believe anything he heard out of the ordinary.

Nevertheless Coggan heard him out and then walked him to the law office door, promising: "I'll be up to the Troy cabin before long, Mr Kelly, and take statements. Tell young Jean to be ready for me. Okay?"

"Thank you," Kelly said, and left, retracing his steps to the foot of the path which led back to the log-built dwelling above.

Climbing his return at a much slower pace than he had descended, Kelly met the top-hatted undertaker and his raw-necked assistant at the half way stage of the track. He stepped aside, to make room for the descending pair — who carried a covered stretcher between them — then, after a muttered exchange of thanks and sympathies, resumed ascending and came upon Jean Troy — who was obviously waiting for him — at the top of the climb. "The sheriff's coming up here shortly," he informed the girl tiredly. "To see you. When's the funeral to be?"

"Three days from now," the girl replied. "What did you tell Matt Coggan?"

Kelly recounted what he had said to the lawman as carefully as he could — fearing how the still only half prepared Jean might take the whole of his story — but she listened to it all quietly enough and, when he had finished speaking, asked: "What do you think Sheriff Coggan will do?"

"Make a show, I guess," Kelly answered. "First he doesn't believe, and second he doesn't want the job. He's your typical small-town sheriff. Clattville is his world — and the only one he wants. Most here won't fault him for that, and nobody will elsewhere."

"It makes you feel so helpless," the girl said resignedly. "Well, nothing will bring Grandfather back. There's the rub. What do you aim to do next, Sam?"

"I'm going to ride to South Hill after the funeral," he replied. "I've business there — at the Union Pacific office."

"I'll have to get a job now," Jean said. "There's hardly a bean between me and the Poor House. I'm coming with you."

Kelly studied her gravely. He didn't consider what she proposed at all a good idea. But he realized that this was hardly the time to tell her so.

4

IN fact Kelly forbore to tell her what he thought about the matter at any time. Jean did indeed have a life to live, and he owed her too much to hurt her feelings by saying that South Hill was no place for an untried girl and that he would prefer to travel there alone anyhow. So he simply acquiesced in the arrangement which she had imposed upon him and let the next three days slip by in the restful but slightly apprehensive tedium of the run up to Pete Troy's funeral.

The one event of interest during those three days was the sale of his meat waggon and the pulling horse. No doubt with an eye to her own benefit now, no less than Kelly's, Jean first charmed Ben Burgess, the general freighter — who was actually holding both the vehicle and the beast on his own premises — and then went in with a woman's boldness and bargained hard until she had secured what was obviously the top price that the man was prepared to pay. She emerged from the deal with three hundred dollars — which was more than Kelly could have reasonably hoped for — and, having paid the twelve dollars due on his doctor's bill, he split what was left down the middle and gave her half, feeling that more than one hundred and forty dollars each would give them both the chance to have a look round and find their feet again in whatever new circumstances presented. In fairness to Jean, she did not wish to take so much from him — saying that a hundred would have more than discharged any debt to her — but he insisted that she take all he offered, for he feared that she might ultimately find the outside world too much for her and want to return to her cabin on the hill. If she did that, residual cash might be needed to make the place habitable again, and this was the only unobtrusive way he knew of providing a possible reserve. Everything there, of course, would depend on the girl's common sense, but he knew that she had plenty of that.

The funeral came. A simple and thinly attended affair, it was dogged by rain and an unseasonable chill. Kelly stood at the graveside and shivered. He had the sad feeling that, despite the slurs cast on Pete Troy's name by Sheriff Coggan, the old trapper had received less than his final due from Clattville. You spoke as you found, and he had found Pete Troy one of the best. That Troy's granddaughter — no fool in judging people — had loved him so well must also say much for his character. Good men often died unappreciated, and Troy could well have been one of them. He had certainly been unlucky in the manner of his death, but that was how it went. They could only pray that he would be remembered by God. At the last, it was the only hope for anybody. Thus dirt rattled on Troy's coffin lid, and a line was drawn under a long life.

Leaving the piece of walled meadow which served Clattville as a cemetery, Kelly and Jean Troy climbed slowly back to the cabin on the hillside. They ate a meal when they got home, but talked only about their departure for South Hill on the morrow and, with the need to be fresh in mind, they went early to their beds, all preparations for a prompt start already made. The night passed as quietly as usual, and they rose at sunup, shunned breakfast — but drank a large pot of coffee — then, after Jean had locked up and pocketed her key, got out their horses from the rough stable off to the left of the drying ground and left the property eastwards. For a few miles they rode their mounts across the high ground of which the Troy hill was a part, but presently they came to falling land and turned northwards down a valley which eventually brought them out onto the prairie which stretched towards the Sweetwater River and beyond.

It was now the noontide of a day as dry and pleasant as the previous one had been dark and inclement and, after stopping to rest the horses and eat some packed food, Kelly and his companion mounted up again and began to cover the ground at a pace that saw them fifty miles beyond Clattville at the day's end. Dog-tired, they slept beside the campfire which Kelly lighted, then rode on again at dawn, arriving in the town of South Hill towards mid-morning.

Jean Troy at once began rubbernecking — since South Hill appeared a genuine metropolis to her, with its town hall, courthouse, emporium, theatre, sale grounds, stockyards, livery barn and much else — but Kelly merely smiled cynically at her interest and suggested that they order some breakfast at the Catfish Restaurant. Here they tied their horses at the hitching rail, then went inside and ate ham and eggs, flapjacks, and bread and honey, finishing up with a pot of coffee so strong that Jean complained it had taken the curl out of her hair. Grinning, Kelly lay back in his chair and lighted his first cigarette of the day; then, exhaling thinned smoke, he nodded at the street outside the plate glass before them and said: "There's your world, Jean. Loads of unwashed folk, sharp trade, snapping dogs and squabbling kids. What do you think of it?"

"Well," the girl said reasonably, "it's not so different from Clattville. There's just more of it."

"I guess you're right at that," Kelly allowed judiciously. "There's a bit more of it down at Cheyenne, and more still along the ironroad at Des Moines. That's as far as I've been, but I'm told there's a real lot of it at Chicago. And the cities back East have to be seen to be believed. Yet who really wants smoke and disease, hey? The land is the true glory, and you had some of the best around Clattville. There's nothing marvellous anywhere,

Jean. Want to know what the key to it all is? Human competence — and just staying alive. Isn't that what you've come to South Hill for?"

She blinked at him.

"What's a job but that?" he inquired.

"Why, yes," she conceded. "But it all seems so — so sudden."

"Always does, Jean," he counselled, "when you're up against something new. I guess we'll have to part shortly."

"Oh, so that's what you're driving at!" she exclaimed. "You do sound a bit like a Dutch uncle at times."

"I must set your head straight," he explained. "I'd be no friend if I didn't do that. You need a room. A boarding house is the best place to live. It isn't so costly as a rule, and you get your privacy there. Don't go into the laundry for a job. That's the hardest of the hard work, and the poorest of the poor pay. Waitressing isn't so bad, and sewing is okay — but the hours are long. Help in a shop is best. Lots of little rests there, and always bargains to be had of the boss. I've never been a man to say anybody should have to work harder than they must."

"Why, Mr Kelly," Jean said archly, "I didn't know you were a lazy man."

"Just telling you," he assured her pleasantly. "It is possible to work yourself to death, and nobody gives a damn. I've laboured under a few slavedrivers. They got rich out of me, and had nothing but contempt for my sweat. Many folk are like that. A fair thing's a fair thing, Jean. It's good for both parties. You see for yourself, and work it out for yourself. Use your own good sense, girl. God forbid that you should ever take any word of mine as gospel!"

She gave him a twisted smile which was also a little shy. "This is where we part?"

"Outside, eh?"

She nodded. He beckoned for the waitress and paid the bill. Then Jean and he stepped out to the sidewalk, where he offered his hand. "Thanks, girl," he said sincerely. "You've been a brick. But this place is really no size, so I guess I'll see you around. For a while anyhow. I'll be in the market for a job too, and my work usually takes me far afield. It appears I've got a fiddlefoot."

"I know," she said, as their hands parted. "Thank you too, Sam. Your money will take the sting out of it."

"Look after yourself," he advised, turning to his horse and freeing it from the rail. He moved to lead it away; then, on the afterthought, paused and added jocularly: "Find yourself a good man, and settle down. Best thing for a woman."

"What's wrong with you?" she responded in the same vein.

"Except everything?" he asked amusedly. "Must make a correction. Find a good wealthy man! One without a three inch patch in his shirt!"

"I sewed it there!" she reminded.

Laughing, he drew his horse up the street, feeling it best to leave her with the last word, and he then walked towards the next intersection ahead, calling to ask directions of a lounging deputy to the Union Pacific's office in this town. "Up Fourth Street," came the reply, the lawman pointing across the corner almost opposite him. "On your right, mister, and two blocks up."

"Got it," Kelly answered. "Thank you."

The deputy flicked a finger in salute, and Kelly made his turn at the intersection and entered Fourth Street. He glanced to where he had been told to look for the U.P. office, and saw it at once — a tall, white-fronted building, with a big brass plate outside the front door and the company flag hanging limply from the pole which slanted over the sidewalk from the pediment above it.

Now Kelly saw a big, high-sided ore waggon approaching him. The presence of the oncoming vehicle forced him over to his right and into the edge of the scene. This caused him a slight irritation, but he was glad a moment later that it had occurred, since a man who was ominously familiar stepped suddenly from the office doorway and glanced at once towards the very ground that Kelly had been traversing only a moment or so previously. The pudgy face, seen twice before now, was unmistakably that of the man who had knifed Kelly beside the waterhole on the prairie. There was a good chance that he had also been the one who had bushwhacked Pete Troy, and that made Kelly bridle and grind his teeth. Lined and truly ugly, the fellow was unquestionably of the white race, and his dark eyes, threatening and muddy, at once singled him out as a man to keep away from. Yet hellish as were the other's looks, he nevertheless had an air of developed intelligence about him, and Kelly sensed that he was no underling and capable of running any show that he had to. Hitching his gunbelt and turning away from the now almost halted watcher, 'pudgy face' walked to the tan gelding which stood at the hitching rail nearest the office door and broke its tie. Then, backing the creature into the street, he stepped up and, fetching to the left, spurred off and headed eastwards, making for the not distant edge of town.

Holding his own features close enough to his mount's neck to keep them obscured — against the possible chance of 'pudgy face' looking back abruptly — Kelly closed in slowly on the ground before the U.P. office and, reaching it, with one eye still upon the horseman receding up street of him, tied his horse where 'pudgy face's' had stood not a minute before. After that, satisfied that his enemy was committed to the country beyond town, Kelly entered the U.P. building and went into the reception hall, where a pretty female clerk was bent over a desk which stood to the left of an oaken door which had the name Taylor Vaughan painted upon it.

The female clerk glanced up, her smile an inviting one and, deciding suddenly to be bold about it, Kelly said: "I saw a stocky man leave the front of this building a minute or two ago. I thought I recognized him from a place I was at a few years back. Can you tell me his name, please?"

"That would have been Victor Bales," came the surprised reply. "He buys in the Union Pacific's timber for Wyoming."

"Thanks. The name's unknown to me. Obviously I mistook Mr Bales for somebody else."

"I've done that myself before today," the girl said, a hint of gravity diluting her smile. "Your business, please?"

"Oh, I'd like to see the manager," Kelly responded. "My name is Sam Kelly. I have a contract to supply head-of-steel with fresh meat."

Averting her eyes, the girl frowned slightly, and Kelly suspected that his name was not unknown to her — which meant she probably also knew that he was contractually in default. "I'll go into Mr Vaughan's office," she said, rising to her feet and smoothing down the seat of her dress, "and ask if he'll see you." Then she slipped out from behind her desk and walked to the door on her right, bowing her head as she knocked on the woodwork.

"Yes?" a deep male voice inquired from within.

Opening the door, the girl put her head into the room beyond. "I have a Mr Sam Kelly out here, sir. He says he's one of our meat contractors. Will you see him?"

"I'll see him."

The girl withdrew her head and stepped back, beckoning.

Kelly moved towards Taylor Vaughan's office. Nodding his thanks to the female clerk, he passed into the room beyond her, finding himself in the presence of a darkly handsome man, with broad shoulders and large head, who dominated a king-sized desk of the plainest kind. As Kelly came to a halt in front of the seated manager, he was aware of the other studying him over the steepled fingers of a pair of particularly big and thickly jointed hands. Kelly had met a number of Union Pacific district managers in his time, and he recognized Taylor Vaughan as typical of the breed — an arrogant, hard-driving man, but essentially shrewd and efficient — and, no lover of men who sought authority, he was instantly disposed to like this man as little as he had done the rest. "Um," Taylor Vaughan grunted disdainfully. "So you're Samuel Kelly?" And the tone of voice, if not the words, deepened his visitor's aversion more than ever.

"Good morning, Mr Vaughan," Kelly said, — politely stressing the seal of the day. "Yes, sir — I'm Sam Kelly."

Vaughan waved a dismissive hand at the girl still lingering near the exit at Kelly's back. "Thank you, Miss Vane," he said briskly. "Please shut the door."

The door clicked shut, and the

manager beckoned Kelly still closer to his desk.

Kelly stayed where he was.

Vaughan let his steepled fingers collapse to rest atop the slight bulge of his abdomen. "Have rather a cheek, don't you, Kelly?"

"Your pardon, Mr Vaughan?"

"You have no business here, man."

"So soon cast off, eh?"

"You failed to deliver fresh meat at John Ranklin's camp," Vaughan said coldly. "Our track engineer was greatly inconvenienced. He got in touch with Head Office at Des Moines, through us. Your meat contract has been terminated in our favour, and Penalty Clause A invoked. Not that our right to redress will be pressed against you. If you'll take the advice of a wiser man, Kelly, you'll go your way this minute, thanking your lucky stars."

"It's about what I expected," Kelly admitted.

"Then why did you come here?"

"More a matter of courtesy than

anything," Kelly replied awkwardly, feeling now that he ought to have stayed away.

"I think not," Taylor Vaughan said scathingly. "I think you're after all you can get."

"I wouldn't call that civil of you," Kelly said sternly.

"Don't ape your betters, my man," the manager said contemptuously. "You were not born to play the gentleman."

"I didn't break my contract deliberately," Kelly flung back hotly. "I've had my share of misfortunes. It would not surprise me if you knew about them."

Vaughan hesitated just perceptibly, something both startled and frightened seeming to appear in his eye for a mere split second. "No. How could I?"

Kelly let his temper have full rein. "Because there was a villain in this building just now who did know about them — damn his soul!"

"Really."

"His name is Victor Bales. I learned it from the girl out in the hall. Don't tell me he didn't visit you!"

"Whether he did or did not is none of your business!" Vaughan returned sharply. "You're trying my patience, Kelly, and I don't like either your expression or the tone of your voice. You seem to be accusing Bales of something. What?"

It was Kelly's turn to hesitate.

"Out with it!"

"He is a timber buyer?"

"There's no crime in that."

"Crime is your word," Kelly reminded. "It gives a roving commission to a man, that's what — a kind of licence to go anywhere he likes and do whatever he pleases without having to provide a close account of it."

"But that's the very nature of the job!" the manager protested. "Bales's task is to buy the almost countless number of ties we use for as little as he can. Where is this leading us, Kelly? What the deuce are you getting at? Or does all this represent the blind malice of a disappointed man?"

Kelly felt himself jerked up short. For a moment there he had been subconsciously sure of himself. But all at once he realized that he was on the verge of openly accusing without proof. The fact that Bales had visited this building — and presumably Vaughan in the process — meant nothing in itself. Equally, the fact that 'pudgy face' was employed by the Union Pacific need prove nothing more than that he could be leading a double life. The parts played by Bales and the manager in Kelly's experience could be as disparate as they appeared in the railroad company's everyday scheme. After all, the two men must spend most of their lives many miles apart and have actual contact only at infrequent intervals. Kelly knew that he was back with the vague and unprovable — had, indeed, let his tongue run away with him in speculations of a reckless and rather mindless kind — and, as he felt the power of his convictions leave him, he saw that he was making a fool of himself rather than achieving anything. Malice had also been the manager's word, and it could be that his visitor, incensed by Vaughan's uncaring and dictatorial manner, had given in to just that. "I'd better go," Kelly said shortly — perceiving instantly that here again he had been guilty of mental clumsiness, for his abruptness had betrayed that he now recognized the weakness of his case and had been slanderously precipitate from the outset.

Taylor Vaughan picked up on it straightaway. "This is shocking!" he declared, springing to his feet and slamming his thick palms down on his desktop. "You can't come in here saying just what you like. Whatever the causes of your failure, Kelly, you failed us, and that's that. You, and no other, are responsible! Seeking to excuse yourself by blaming another is reprehensible in the extreme. I shall report this incident where it will do you the most harm — at Head Office.

You'll never work for the Union Pacific again. Now get out of here!"

Kelly withdrew from the manager's office. He looked at once towards Miss Vane's desk on the left and saw from her secret smile that she had heard and enjoyed his verbal spanking from Taylor Vaughan and, rejoining his horse at the hitching rail outside, stood humiliated and smarting. What a mess he had made of things, for he certainly hadn't come here to stir up trouble. He had let the influences present gain control of him. Yet, through it all, he suddenly felt that Taylor Vaughan's haughty rage had been more the product of relief than justly angered propriety. Deep within him there remained the conviction that there was more here than met the eye, and he was sure that if he went into the business further he would make discoveries far bigger than any he had dreamed of so far. Here again there wasn't much of a tangible nature to go on, but there was enough to make him feel obliged to justify himself. He would try to solve this business concerning Victor Bales and Taylor Vaughan by his own powers. After all, he was at a loose end, had money in his saddlebags, and owed the shade of Pete Troy an earthly revenge for the bullet which had hurled him into the next world ahead of time. In his secret heart, Kelly knew that some such notion had been with him for the last day or two, but it had crystallized now and he was committed. His humiliation by Taylor Vaughan had achieved that much, so his visit to the Union Pacific office had been far from entirely wasted.

Kelly freed his horse and mounted up. He rode down Fourth Street and soon came to the place where the beaten way thinned into the prairie east of town. Now he headed out into the plain and, spurring to a gallop, began travelling over the guessed at route that Victor Bales had probably used when leaving South Hill. Given that Bales had shown no sign of being in any great hurry — and that he could not in those circumstances have ridden very far as yet — it was probable that, if Kelly's gamble on direction were valid, a climb to the summit of some prairie eminence not too far away would still reveal his presence at this point or that on the not too distant grassland. If it didn't, the hunter would just have to backtrack and undertake a search for trace. That would obviously slow up his plans, but everything about this start was speculative anyway.

Kelly galloped hard, keeping up the pace for three or four miles. The gentle rolling of the prairie was fairly uniform on every hand, and he saw no hillock of the kind he sought at the time he wished it most. Thus, forced on at a slower pace for another mile or two, he finally saw what he was seeking over to his right.

Turning, he cantered his mount to the foot of the high spot and then climbed the animal to its top, settling there and lifting in his stirrups to gaze out across the flower-clad fields of the prairie spring, seeking any movement upon the semi-arc of green that formed the next few miles of the country ahead. Fearing that he was about to discover that his impromptu calculations were at fault and there was no rider on the land between north-east and southwest, Kelly was pleasantly surprised to glimpse the horseman he sought trotting down exactly the line which he had imagined. Then, raising his eyes and guessing again, he thought that Bales's destination might well turn out to be the area of higher land which he could now make out due east of him and well short of the skyline. It looked just the kind of remote and rugged spot for which a man of dubious connections would be likely to head. It figured, then, that Bales and his tan-coloured horse could be on their way to a hideout.

Leaving the summit, Kelly sent his mount racing down the hillside and back to the lower ground. Holding the position of his now invisible quarry in his mind's-eye, he kept up the gallop until his horse started blowing and he knew that he must have reduced the gap between him and the rider ahead very considerably. Slowing, though not too much, he pressed on for a further half an hour, feeling the loom of the higher ground before him and picking out the details of its steep banks, dark gullies, tree-clad ridges and crumbling cliffs, everything ruggedly bunched and tumbled under a sun-gold sky which was fretted with cirrus.

On the level of the plain, a grassy crest now broke Kelly's field of vision. Upon its near side, the figure of his quarry appeared and climbed into prominence. Seeking the shadows, Kelly watched the other cross the green ridge and dip out of sight behind it. After that the pursuer went at it hard again and soon reached the climb himself, swinging down just below the summit and completing his ascent on bounding feet.

Dropping onto his stomach, Kelly parted the long grass atop the ridge and looked down through the gap that he had made into the hollow at the base of the crest's reverse side. He saw that Bales had just finished crossing the low and entered the bottom of a gully that climbed the steep bank beyond for three hundred feet and more before vanishing into upper shadows where the bank joined the higher formations of the land mass which Kelly had seen initially from the top of his first climb several miles back.

Convinced that his man was up against a land barrier of some magnitude and wouldn't be going much further, Kelly stayed where he was until his quarry had finished climbing the gully and merged with the upper scene. Then, at his most wary now — since he could not ignore the possibility that his movements were already being watched from the heights before him — Kelly retreated to where his horse stood, led the animal over the ridge and remounted on the reverse slope, riding quickly down into the low and then across its grassy bottom to the foot of the gully up which Bales and his tan gelding had recently climbed.

Alighting from his saddle again, Kelly tipped back his head and looked up the gully. It was an ugly scar and clearly carried water through much of the year. Kelly did not doubt his ability to climb it on horseback, but he reckoned that, if anything should go wrong and he were forced to descend it in haste, he would be safer on foot than coming down those slippery grades over four horseshoes. So, if he were going up there, he had better do it on his two feet, since it also occurred to him now that a man being chased off the heights — presumably by other men afoot — would have the better chance of getting clear and away if he had a horse hidden near the bottom of the descent.

Kelly led his mount into a nearby notch at the base of the slope. Here the animal should be fairly well hidden from both above and below. Now Kelly ground-tied the brute, then returned to the foot of the gully. Keeping his wits about him every moment of the time, he started climbing, and he progressed with some effort but no great difficulty, arriving after a few minutes in the widely fanned inlet that topped the gully amidst a spread of bushes high above. Here he paused yet again, studying the broken clay and dull rock of this drainage spot, and he saw that numerous horses must have scrambled over it in recent weeks. The tracks left above this place were no less plain, and he followed one of them up and onwards through the bushes for another ten or fifteen yards to where it broke left and stopped on the lip of a considerable hollow that was largely encircled by live-oak and pine scrub. A single entrance, worn out by untold generations of game, served the hollow — which contained grass and spring-waters at its centre — and Kelly immediately glimpsed about a dozen horses milling slowly around the eye of brightness and ripping at the graze that ringed it in a languid manner.

Touching the pistol on his right hip, Kelly knew that he must be getting close to whatever kind of hideout was located up here, and he began climbing again where boots had broken away the moss which covered a form of natural stair and traced a fully visible path up the slope which linked the hollow with a rockface about fifty feet above that was part of the jagged ridge in which these heights ended. He scrambled still further upwards, and found himself almost as high as he could go. He must be getting very near whatever danger was present, and a challenge might reach him at any second. It was getting a little scary.

Kelly saw a screen of growth a short distance beyond him and to his left. Doubling low, he catfooted towards it, sending odd fragments of crumbled stone out from beneath his soles. Then the hedge of dead vines and struggling ash brought him to a halt, and he stood gasping to recover his breath as he heard bursts of coarse male laughter drawing to him from behind the extinct tendrils and failing greenery before him. After that, his lungs easing, he pressed up to the shielding veil and, using a careful right hand, opened a hole through it and partially exposed the base of the granite wall beyond.

Now, pistol half drawn — just in case — he put an eye to the aperture and sought whatever was there to be seen on the other side of it.

5

KELLY found himself looking almost directly into a cave. Near enough sure now that his presence up here had not so far been detected, he relaxed a trifle and let his revolver slide back fully to rest. He fixed all his attention on the interior of the cave, where he made out a good number of figures sitting in the shadows of the rocky hole and either drinking whisky-laced coffee out of tin cups or smoking pipes and cigarettes. The gusts of laughter repeated, and it was clear that a huge joke was being enjoyed by all, with the pudgy-faced Victor Bales self-importantly holding court at the centre of it. "I tell you," he insisted, "it's got near enough as bad as that!"

"You can't mean it, Vic!" another speaker protested incredulously. "Do you want us to believe that our white brothers are so stupid they're fixin' to arrest Sitting Bull for our play acting?"

"That's just what I'm telling you, Avery," Bales responded. "Our play acting is a bigger take-in than you think."

"What now?" somebody else jeered. "It'd suit me fine if the Army threw Sitting Bull into the stockade. Now Crazy Horse has gone to the Happy Hunting Grounds, there's only that old hellion left to stir the pot!"

"A few more of our raids," Bales guffawed, "and I shouldn't wonder that's how it will turn out. Taylor Vaughan told me, not two hours ago, the Army's watching Sitting Bull's lodge night and day. General Miles can't figure out how so much is happening when Sitting Bull gets no visitors. Miles won't even have that medicine man, Yellow Bird, near the big chief — in case it's him sending out messages by what's known as mental telepathy."

"Did you ever hear such nonsense?" asked the man to whom Bales had been addressing himself.

"I never did," Bales admitted. "But there you are, Collins. When folk get rattled, they'll believe any rubbish."

"About time we hit again," a fourth speaker prompted.

"That's what Vaughan intends," Bales returned. "He wants us to make a few more quick strikes in this neck-of-the-woods, and then fade out. He's moving down to Topeka before long. Got himself a transfer to the Kansas Pacific. Says we can follow him, and start up again down there. He figures we'd do best out of a spell of train robbing. Maybe add in a few stage coaches too. We'd see how we went on anyhow."

"I'm not complaining, Vic."

"Didn't say you were, Dempsey," Bales said airily. "What's there to complain about? We're all dollars in!"

"But we aren't down there yet," Dempsey observed. "Where do we make our next raid up here?"

"West of this spot," Bales answered. "Little place called Renton — about twenty miles from South Hill. Not far away. The bank there's got fat on mining and cattle. They've never had a robbery, and Taylor Vaughan says the law is real slack. The sheriff spends most of his time fishing and caring for fat widow women."

"Don't that go to prove it, Vic?" a fifth voice piped. "We're in the wrong job! I ain't cared for a fat widow woman in far too long! How do I get me a star?"

"You get yourself a star, Jack Jeyes," yet another speaker warned, "and you'll be swinging on it come Sunday week. Y'hear now?"

"Aw, shut up squawking, Jessup, y'long-legged toad!" Jeyes advised bitterly. "Ain't good for a real man to be stuck with a seedy mob like this month in and month out. Wish I'd fetched my cousin Ruth along. What she can't do for a man!"

"Don't worry yourself, Jack!" Bales commented sarcastically. "Cousin Ruth is doing plenty for the other guys in your absence."

"She wouldn't!" Jeyes yelped.

"Yes, she would, sonny!" Bales affirmed amidst a new outburst of haw-hawing. "They all do. Think on Renton! It isn't heaven, but it is money. And what else can you spend? Cousin Ruth will still be there when you get home."

"You're a skunk, Vic!" Jeyes declared.

"Natural to these parts," Bales acknowledged inconsequentially. "That makes you a puppy, I shouldn't wonder! Anyhow, we're going to Renton real soon now — and that does include you, Jack boy, so get ready to button your britches."

"You hear me say otherwise, Victor?"

"I hadn't better!"

The listening Kelly had been pulling faces to himself and enjoying both the dialogue and what he had been learning with such remarkable ease;

but then it all ended in a kind of disillusionment as the muzzle of a pistol ground against his backbone. "What are you snouting in there for?" a youthful voice demanded nastily. "Who the tarnation are you? What are you up to?"

Kelly's mind raced. He'd got to be both quick and smart about this or he was done for. But he did have a strong impression that he was dealing with an inexperienced kid who was uncertain about his place in things. "Aren't you being a mite premature with that hogleg, boy?" he asked acidly over his shoulder. "Have the goodness to let me back out of this hedge. Vic will skin you if I come by a hole in my pelt!"

"Huh?"

The pressure of the gun muzzle eased on Kelly's spine, and he sensed that he had put his challenger in two minds. Spinning to his left, Kelly whirled out of the growth, making a fast draw as he did so, and he clapped the barrel of his Colt against the head of the leonine but not markedly intelligent-looking young man who had crept up behind him. The 'buffaloed' kid fell in a manner which suggested that he was likely to remain senseless for the next hour, and all should have been well and the danger averted, but the kid's revolver went off with a sharp crack as it bounced away from his nerveless hand and Kelly's discovery by the men in the cave was thus ensured.

Putting up his gun, Kelly thought only of escape. He began fleeing downhill, and was soon conscious of a confused shouting at his back. His feet moved faster and faster and, his running steps almost out of control, he reached the base of the upper slope before he was fully aware of it. Only just managing to catch himself, he avoided going over the brink of the hollow which contained the horses by inches at most, skidded round to his left, tripping dangerously, and had barely recovered his stride when a single shot thumped out of his wake and a bullet tore through foliage somewhere above his head and brought a leaf or two floating down.

Through the bushes he sped at the top of the gully, stumbling again on the rock which protruded from the bald earth which formed the inlet area; and then it was down into those steeps that he had earlier feared while looking upwards from the grass below, the watercourse funnelling into slippery narrows which set his smooth soles skating. Down — down! Faster — faster! His backside struck the ground and he tobogganed several yards on his canvas seat, the heat of the friction thus generated scorching the soft skin of his buttocks. After that his right shoulder struck a lump of rock which thrust out into his path and the impact spun him completely round.

He entered a new stage of progress. This carried him several times head-over-heels. There was pain enough to bear, and danger to his consciousness too, but this form of somersaulting motion was abruptly checked as he flung out full length upon an acutely angled bed of sand and his soles drove against an upthrusting step of rock that crossed the floor of the gully from side to side and created a physical feature off which the run-off waters from above must leap out into a considerable fall during times of flood.

Lying prone, Kelly thrust himself off the bottom of the deep-worn channel and peered dizzily back and upwards. He couldn't see Bales and company yet, but picked up the ringing of their feet as they lumbered down the upper part of the hill towards the gully. Up far too soon for his own good, Kelly gazed to the front again and jumped over the step which had originally brought him up short, landing shakily in the most acutely angled part of the drain beneath his checkpoint, but desperation saved his wavering tread and, seconds later — at a place where the gully deepened almost to his own height — he was able to fling out his hands to either side and regain his balance entirely. With this generally steadying effect came the clearing of his head, and after that his ability to leap and bound normally came back. Thus, in a now fully disciplined manner, he entered a long phase of light-footed descent and saw the grass below rising at him apace.

He was only yards from the bottom of the gully when gunfire began to volley down at him from far above. Lead skipped and ricocheted about him, and he felt his heart almost literally rise into his mouth; but he did not look round and up again, since he was reasonably certain that the men up there had little idea of what he looked like and would be able to speculate only in the vaguest of manners as to his possible identity. Even Bales must be at a loss so far — particularly as the fellow had good cause to believe him dead — and, so long as the badman did not get a clear look at his features, he was sure that he would be able to get away from this spot and nobody any the wiser as to anything about him for the moment.

With a veritable hail of slugs still singing and dancing around him, Kelly entered and sprang out of the gully's base, turning left and ducking into the shelter of the land before haring towards the niche in which he had left his horse. Coming to the brute, he seized its head and backed it out of the indent, swinging it to the right now and stepping astride it. Then, shaking the sweat from his brow and gulping air, he struck with his rowels and headed southwards, working up to full gallop inside twenty yards.

Guns went on banging from high up and to his rear, but he heard nothing of the bullets any more and soon felt confident that he was clear and away. There was an instant temptation to ease off a little — especially as he considered the delay the badmen must now suffer while bringing their horses down from the height — but a deeper intelligence advised him to press his advantage to the full, and he kept his horse at the maximum for the next fifteen minutes, putting a number of miles between him and the position of the hideout before reducing speed and giving his lathered mount the chance to make a partial recovery from its extreme efforts.

Before long Kelly swung into the west. The land over here was far more broken than it had been to the east of him. Now he brought guile into the business, taking full advantage of rockland and dusthill, and within the hour he knew that he had covered his tracks so skilfully that any hunt which Bales might now be leading would never trace through in the hours of daylight remaining. In fact every glance that Kelly had so far cast back had revealed empty country in his wake, and he could not help wondering whether the badmen had simply accepted his escape and left it at that. When the inertia produced by doubt was taken into account, this possibility was stronger than might have seemed likely at first glance. After all he could have been no more than a nosey traveller who chanced on the outlaws' hideout while travelling the plains. This, too, was just possible.

But, if the badmen could be plagued by uncertainties, Kelly was forced to turn to and recognize his own. He had heard about that forthcoming raid on the not too distant town of Renton — and had received the idea that it was to be carried out very soon — yet he could not be absolutely sure about that. The obvious course seemed to ride at once to Renton and tell what he had overheard; but he had also gathered that the town was cursed with a lazy sheriff. The man would want accurate information or nothing, and that didn't encourage Kelly to make for Renton there and then.

Perhaps it was more important that he return to South Hill. The authorities there ought to be told that Taylor Vaughan, the Union Pacific manager, was the brains behind the apparent Indian raids and other depredations which had lately been taking place in central Wyoming. But what precisely to do about that was also a problem. For he could see himself getting laughed to scorn if he tried to get Vaughan arrested on the little that he knew at present. In order to make any real use of what he had so far learned, he would need the help of somebody with genuine power who also had the perception and fearlessness to accept the limited evidence available and at least neutralize Taylor Vaughan until the case against him became irrefutable. The help Kelly envisaged would, then, need to be of a very sophisticated kind and clearly outside any force which he could presently influence or command. And that amounted to a problem which made him shake his head, for it all seemed rather hopeless at the minute. Touching right rein, he turned his horse in the direction of South Hill and forced his mind to relax. He would spend his night in the town where the major evil was situated. This business couldn't be as impossible as it seemed right now. He would probably achieve most by forgetting about it for the minute. It never did any good to keep pressing where nothing would yield.

He re-entered South Hill from the west and during the early evening. He had had a hard day, but he realized that his horse had had a harder one, so he put the brute in at the livery barn and gave orders for it to receive the best treatment that money could buy. Then he sauntered along to the Catfish Restaurant — where he and Jean Troy had eaten that morning — knocked back a steak and vegetables, inhaled the whole of a macaroni pudding, drank coffee by the large cup, smoked a cigarette or two, admired the waitress, and finally put his mind to the matter of where he was to spend the night. He could go back to the livery barn, and beg a spot in the hay loft, but he had means enough to sleep comfortably, so he decided to do just that.

When asked, the waitress informed him that a Mrs Alice Baines ran a respectable boarding house just a few doors further down the main street. Kelly walked to the lodging place, requested a room, and was given his key and number. Then the humourless Mrs Baines took his dollar and showed him the way upstairs. After that she left him to it; but he found his room without difficulty and dumped himself into the threadbare armchair beside the hearth. Replete and belching, he reached up and took an old newspaper off the mantelpiece, opening it at the Cheyenne gossip; but there was nothing written there that interested him and he soon took off his clothing and went to bed, where he lay staring at the ceiling as the late spring evening wore itself into the pale and starry darkness which passed for night as the season moved towards the year's longest day.

Tired as he was, he couldn't sleep. He tried every trick he knew to induce slumber, but sleep would not come. There had been a lot of excitement during the day, and he realized that he was overstimulated. Nor had he helped matters by eating too much, guzzling an excess of coffee, and smoking strong tobacco. There was another form of discomfort too. He could not rid himself of the underlying fear that Vic Bales had ridden into town during the evening and met Taylor Vaughan. If Bales had given the Union Pacific manager an account of what had happened out at the gang's hideout, it would have emerged — this way or that — that he, Kelly, had called in at the U. P. office that morning. Thus, learning that his enemy was still alive, Bales would be hunting Kelly again. There was a definite possibility that Vaughan — an important man who no doubt had his sources — already knew that Kelly had returned to town and could have apprised his henchman as to the fact. This could even mean that another attack on the meat contractor's life was imminent and, though Kelly felt no sense of an immediate threat, he could not dismiss the chance that Bales would seek him out in his bed and try to murder him there. The very risk of that was enough to keep a guy awake.

But Kelly did sleep in the end. He went off during the early hours and slept through until noisy activity in the house below warned him that a new day had begun. Duty bound to leave his room before nine o'clock — when the housework began — he got up in a hurry and threw his clothes back on, leaving the boarding house with last night's needless worries driven to the back of his mind.

Aware that he didn't smell too sweet and was a bit of a sight, Kelly went at once to the barbershop, where he had a hot bath, shave, and trim. These treatments made him considerably more presentable — which turned out to be a very good thing indeed — for he was no sooner out of the barber's establishment than he ran into Jean Troy on the street. The girl was dressed in her best female garments, had a shopping basket on her left arm, and had the look about her of a happy woman whose life had taken on a purpose. "Sam!" she exclaimed, her eyes lighting up still further at the sight of him.

"Hello, Jean," he greeted. "How goes it?"

"I've got a job."

"Congratulations!" he applauded. "That was quick work! Don't get drunk and lose it, will you?"

"That sounds like you!" she laughed. "I'm working for the judge."

"The judge?"

"Judge Harrison Reed."

"Good heavens!" Kelly exclaimed, turning his eyes upwards in pious contemplation of the pink-tinged morning clouds. "What would your late grandpa have said?"

"I went for a room at the Brent boarding house," she explained. "Violet Brent, the daughter of the house, said I was far too nice a girl to be looking for a room at their place. So I told her that I was just starting out in the world and looking for a job. She said she thought she could help me in that, and she sent me to Judge Reed's house on Second Street, where I was interviewed by Ethel Colby, the judge's housekeeper. She employed me there and then, as the trainee housemaid. The judge is a fine old man, and Mrs Colby is the kindest and nicest of ladies. A real motherly soul. I've a lovely room to sleep in, and I eat like a queen. What more could any girl ask?"

"Sure sounds like you've fallen on your feet okay," Kelly enthused. "I'm happy for you, Jean! It's good to know you've been taken care of in style!"

"What about you, Sam?" she inquired, her demeanour more serious now.

"Oh, this business of being in and out of work is a familiar one to me," Kelly replied, for he had suddenly glimpsed a possible path to that special kind of help which he had seen himself as needing yesterday afternoon but been more or less forced to forget about since because it all seemed so near a practical impossibility. "The fact is, Jean, I've got a real corker of a task on right now." And he went on to give her a succinct account of all that had happened to him after he had left her the day before.

"That explains it," Jean said, when he had finished speaking, a reflective expression on her face.

"Explains what?"

"The judge had a dinner guest last night," she hurried on — "a very handsome man who seemed to take a shine to me. He asked a few questions, and appeared genuinely interested in what had recently happened to me over at Clattville. Also in how you and I rode here."

"Are you talking about Taylor Vaughan?" Kelly hazarded.

"Of course, Sam."

"Did that skunk mention having met me?"

"In passing, yes," she said, her eyes pleading. "Oh, Sam! I can't believe Mr Taylor Vaughan is a crook and master of crooks. You must be mistaken!"

"I'm not mistaken," Kelly said grimly. "He's a clever son-of-Satan, and a crafty one too. You haven't gone and fallen in love with him, have you?"

"Sam!" she exclaimed, blushing.

"Have you ever been in love, Jean?" The girl shook her head, gaze falling.

"You're due for it, honey," he said matter-of-factly. "It happens to us all. Part of Nature's work, I guess."

"It happened to you?"

"Sure did," Kelly said wryly. "She was a schoolma'am. I was all of twelve years old — and it hurt like hell!"

"You started young, Mr Kelly."

"No such luck!" he returned dryly. "These things have to work both ways. Teacher took a ruler to my knuckles when she saw me sizing up her bustle."

"Sam, you're shocking!"

"You wanted to see more of life," he reminded. "This is it. You're in the front row, Jean. It starts with a fond kiss and ends with rocking a cradle. For a girl, that is. It's marvellous, and then some. But it's real dangerous too. So just be warned when the guy steers for a clinch!"

"Men are enemies?"

There was a twinkle in his eye as he gave his chin a jerk.

"Even you?"

"I'm a friendly one. But — you sure are a pretty girl, and I'm not so different from the rest."

"This morning?" she queried perceptively.

"This morning I need something else of you, Jean."

"What's that?"

He paused, his brow wrinkled and his teeth clenching, all too aware of the enormity of what he was about to ask. "An introduction to Judge Reed."

"A what?" Jean Troy blinked, clearly unable to believe her ears. "You can't be serious, Sam!"

"Dead serious," he assured her. "You want your grandpa's murder avenged, don't you?"

"Yes, but — "

"That being so, I've got to start putting the pinch on Vic Bales and his bad bunch," Kelly interrupted. "I also need to have Taylor Vaughan watched. I must get the truth about those renegades through to others before the law will step in and put a stop to what's going on. I occasionally talk big, Jean, but I'm just a nobody. Who's going to believe a word I say if I can't put it beside the kind of evidence that needs no swearing? I'm out to get there how I can, honey, and the way looks to be through you. Savvy?"

"This is crazy, Sam!" the girl announced flatly. "It's simply out of the question! Can't you grasp that? I'm a brand new face in the judge's house, and Mrs Colby insists that I treat him like a god. Don't you see? She'll put me out of the door right straightaway if I ask something of His Honour that she regards as being altogether too much!"

"Sure," Kelly said, sighing drearily, "we're a pair of nobodies. But if I'm ready to get my head stove in — so's to save a few hides over in Renton — can't you be the same?"

"You ask too much, Sam!" Jean now returned resolutely. "I won't see my future risked on a tall story and a slight acquaintance. Good gracious, man! I can't credit that you're really as blindly selfish as you seem. If you want those outlaws properly chased, go to the sheriff with your tale. He's the man for the job!"

"And have him display the same attitude concerning Taylor Vaughan as you're showing?" Kelly asked unhappily. "I wish I didn't understand how you feel; but I do. You're scared from top to bottom. First because you don't truly believe me, but mainly because these educated folk are too big in your eye. The greatest of us are only men and women, Jean, and when they turn on the rest of us, they, too, have to be stopped. 'S-a-fact!"

"Perhaps," Jean said obstinately. "But you must find another — "

A shot cracked out from nearby. The bullet holed the cuff of Kelly's jacket, passing on to burn the hindquarters of a grey gelding that stood tied to a hitching rail only a few feet away. The horse bucked hugely, venting a frantic neighing sound, and its tugging weight broke the tie which held it to the rail, allowing it to wheel away to its right and go stampeding crazily up the street, its near side haunch striking Jean Troy as it swept by and throwing her sideways.

The girl hit the ground with some violence, and rolled several times before coming to a stop. Kelly gazed at her still form, mouth and eyes shocked wide open — then started running towards her.

6

DROPPING to his knees beside the fallen Jean, Kelly turned her off her face. He was trembling with anxiety, and had almost forgotten the initial cause of her accident. But he was sharply reminded of it when the hidden gun spoke once more and lead whipped at his hair and then whacked the boardwalk a short distance away.

Now Kelly plucked out his pistol and thumbed back its hammer. Head tipped to one side, he let a glaring eye pick out the spot at which the explosions had occurred. Then, beside the angle of the wall where an alley opened on the right and between two stores about twenty yards away, he saw enough of a man's face to be sure that the murderous gunman was again Vic Bales.

Upping his Colt, Kelly snapped off a shot at the bulging cheek that showed itself, determined to get in an off putter as he sensed that the fleshy killer was about to trigger for the third time. After that he jacked himself erect and, setting his feet apart, fanned off the remaining four shells in his cylinder at the spot where the segment of fat face had just been snatched from sight. His bullets went where he aimed them. They shattered both the woodwork of the corner and the cast iron drainpipe behind it, throwing splinters all over the place, but he received no intimation of scoring a hit and became certain that he had missed when he picked up sounds of a lumbering run which could only be the would-be killer in flight. He would have pelted after his man, and was on the brink of doing so, when Jean Troy stirred and pushed her upper body off the ground, turning dazed eyes up and round towards him.

Kelly thrust his empty gun away. Hands outstretched, he moved back to the girl. "Are you all right, Jean?" he asked tautly.

"I — I think so," she responded faintly. "I feel sure there are no bones broken."

"I'll take you to the doctor's place."

"No, Sam — I'm okay," she assured him, pushing aside his hands and rising unsteadily to prove it.

Straightening up with her, Kelly stepped up close and put an arm around her as her knees wobbled. "I'm going to take you home anyhow," he said in tones that brooked no argument.

"I've got shopping to do, Sam."

"Too bad," he said flatly.

"Mrs Colby may not like it."

"Mrs Colby can go and fry," Kelly responded, picking up the basket which the girl had dropped when she fell. "Can you walk all right?"

She took a couple of firm steps, as he moved with her, proving that she could.

"Where, Jean?"

She nodded northwards, up the street.

Supporting her closely, Kelly carefully matched her uneven steps, letting the rate at which they covered the ground be entirely her choice. He was pleased with the direction they were taking, for it gave him the chance to glance into the alley behind the damaged corner when they came to it. The ground there was indeed empty, and Kelly had no doubt that Vic Bales had by now regained safety a fair distance away. Well, the attack had been no real surprise to him; it was simply that he had let Bales catch him off guard. It just went to prove how easy it was to become diverted — and amounted to a stern warning; since he had no doubt that Bales would keep trying.

Made tightly vigilant by that thought, Kelly wished he could reload his revolver, but it nevertheless seemed wiser to go on with Jean as he had been going. There were people around now — folk who had hurriedly taken cover while the bullets were flying — but they kept their distance and did no more than peer curiously at Kelly and the shaken girl. That suited Kelly admirably, for he didn't want the good citizens falling over Jean and himself in what would be well-intentioned but useless efforts to be of help.

Entering Second Street, they came almost at once to the house which Jean Troy pointed out as that belonging to Judge Harrison Reed. It occupied ground on the left, was built of bricks, and had obviously been conceived by an architect who had received his training in Europe. That the dwelling had not been erected yesterday was proved by the masses of wistaria which had accumulated on its front wall, and the garden — with its worn crazy paving and dense clumps of flowering shrubs — also had a long-established look about it.

Kelly pushed open Judge Harrison Reed's front gate. Then he assisted his companion along to the judge's door, where he pulled the handle of the bell and set up a noisy ringing in the hall beyond. The door opened to them almost immediately, and Kelly saw before them a round-faced, greying woman, who wore a slight expression of strain about her pale blue eyes and had a wide, thick-lipped mouth that displayed an instant readiness to smile — though the smile died at once when she noted Jean Troy's pallor and saw the dusty state of the girl's clothing. "Whatever has happened to you, Jean?" she asked, her slightly worn teeth catching at her lower lip.

"It's nothing to get alarmed about, ma'am," Kelly assured her. "Jean here got knocked over when a horse took fright. She's shook up some, but I don't reckon there's any real harm done."

"Bring her inside," the woman ordered. "Quickly now!"

Kelly eased his companion into the hall. He glimpsed a tiled floor and walls that were decorated with a variety of art pieces. The house had the sweet smells of soap and polish about it, and rays of sunlight fell through a skylight that was placed above the landing which crossed the middle hall. A dog barked at the rear of the dwelling; and then a black-suited man who was tall, spare, slightly stooped, and very elegant after his white-bearded and stern-eyed fashion, stepped out of a room on the left and looked inquiringly towards the woman standing before the two entrants from the front step. "What is it, Ethel?" he asked, the authority in his voice matching the force of his presence.

"Jean has been hurt, sir," the middle aged woman explained. "It seems she was knocked over by a runaway horse."

"Well, Jean?" the tall man demanded, his abruptness belied by the kindly light in his eyes.

"A shot had been fired, Judge," Jean Troy answered dully.

"It nicked the horse," Kelly added hurriedly. "Some clown was trying to drygulch me."

"Was he now?" Harrison Reed mused. "This town is becoming dangerous. We must put a stop to that." He turned back into the room from which he had recently stepped forth. "Bring the girl in here, Mrs Colby."

Kelly obeyed the older woman's beckoning finger, and steered Jean into a white walled room that was indeed generally white — from the fireplace to the curtains, and even to the polar bearskin rugs around the floor — and, at a sign from the judge, who had just taken up a stance before the hearth, seated the girl in a thickly cushioned leather armchair close to a glass-fronted bookcase.

"Give her a glass of brandy, Mrs Colby," the judge ordered, and his housekeeper nodded and went to the drinks tray standing on the sideboard.

"I — I really am all right, thank you," Jean Troy muttered.

Harrison Reed ignored her. He was plainly satisfied that he knew best about her condition. "Do you know who I am, young man?" he asked, addressing himself to Kelly.

"You must be Judge Harrison Reed,

sir," Kelly answered. "Jean and I know each other. I was helped by her and her grandpa, when I got knifed by a villain named Victor Bales near a little place south of here."

"I think I heard something of this over last evening's dinner table," the judge observed. "You will be — ?"

"Sam Kelly, Judge."

"I did tell you about him, sir," Jean said.

The judge nodded. "I fear you're a stormy petrel, young fellow."

"How's that again?" Kelly asked.

"A manner of speech," the judge replied dismissively, frowning. "You named the man who stabbed you, Kelly. I understood from what Jean said that your attacker was an Indian."

"That's what I believed at first," Kelly admitted, now perceiving that, against all the odds and in the most natural of manners, he had been given the opportunity to inform somebody who had real power — and was also learned and discriminating — of what he knew regarding the renegade guns. "The fact is, Judge, I know a heap about some doings that throw a mighty poor light on our white race and one member of it who, I think, is no stranger to you."

"Indeed. And who's that?"

"Taylor Vaughan."

"The Union Pacific manager?" the judge queried. "Yes, Taylor Vaughan is well known to me. I'd almost call him a personal friend. I take it that you're accusing Mr Vaughan of something grave?"

"Very grave."

"Go on."

"It's my belief that he's running a bunch of crooks who're playing a double game," Kelly explained. "It seems to me some of them go and dress up as Indians and make a nuisance of themselves around this remote township or that; and then, as soon as the male inhabitants get steamed up and set out to chase them, the other guys, all white and normal, ride in and sting the town their pals have so craftily weakened."

"Pshaw!" Harrison Reed exclaimed, half amazed and half mocking. "Am I expected to believe this?"

"You'd better, Judge," Kelly said bluntly — "because it's the truth. I even know where the gang is hiding out — and that their next target is Renton?"

The judge raised a vaguely indicating thumb. "Over there?"

"That Renton, yes," Kelly answered. "Sure, it wants some swallowing. But, if you want, I'll swear on a stack of bibles that it's the truth."

"That fallible thing the truth," the judge mused; philosophically. "I've encountered many a man who was sure that he was purveying the truth, yet was still mistaken. It has even happened to me."

"It's happened to me too," Kelly confessed. "But I'm certain sure about this."

Harrison stood rooted, his eyes fixed upon the floor, and he stood thus for the better part of a minute, what was visible of his face betraying the intensity of the battle that was going on inside him. Then, glancing up, slit-eyed and grim, he said: "I dare not ignore this. It could rebound at a later date and be the finish of me. Yet I have to be absolutely certain that what you have told me is right before I dare act upon it. Even a territorial judge — or perhaps a territorial judge more than anybody — has to recognize the prevalence of false witness, whether accidental or deliberate. The Union Pacific is among the largest and most powerful business organizations in our country today. Many of the men most highly placed in government have connections with the railroad. Nobody is above the law, Kelly — and I'll lay down my life for that concept if I must — but even such as I need more evidence than I've had from you before invoking the law against a servant of those who have the power to break us."

"I figured it might be like that,"

Kelly said. "I reckon you're being extraordinarily honest with me."

"Your interest could be malicious, Kelly."

"Yeah," Kelly conceded dryly, "a knife in the back sure makes a guy salty, Judge. Yet I'd have you believe my motive force here is mainly what happened to Jean's grandfather. The bullet that cut him down was meant for me."

Though continuing to look uncertain, Harrison Reed slowly nodded his head. "There's one way I might be able to help us both and also be able to cover us both."

"What's that?"

"Make you a servant of the law."

"Now you are talking, by heck!" Kelly breathed.

"I am indeed," the judge agreed, looking hard at Mrs Colby, who had been holding the glass while giving Jean Troy small sips of brandy to drink. "Kindly take the girl through to the kitchen, Ethel. I wish to speak privately with Mr Kelly."

"Yes, sir," the housekeeper said, setting aside the brandy glass and helping Jean out of the armchair in which she was slumped. Then the pair of them left the room, and their footfalls faded up the hall and into the back of the house, where the closure of a door in their wake finally cut off all sound of their talk and movements.

With hands linked behind his back and head bowed, Harrison Reed began pacing back and forth in front of the white marble fireplace. "Kelly," he suddenly began, matching the rhythms of his speech to those of his tread, "this isn't going to be as easy for you as a simple yes or no. I must ask you now to tell me your full story, leaving out no detail. This could be trying for you — even tedious — but I must know exactly what I'm assisting. Do you understand? I want every detail."

"Got you, Judge," Kelly responded, inwardly confessing to himself that he was getting fed up with chewing this business over; but he did realize that, aside from anything else, it was only fair that he should do what Harrison Reed asked, since the judge had little more than what Jean had told him to go by so far. So he spent the next quarter of an hour recounting all that had happened to him since he had first spotted those make believe redskins chopping down the telegraph wires to the east of Clattville up to this morning's incident here in South Hill. As Kelly fell silent, the judge sat down on the nearest chair and, after a few moments of reflection, said: "Yes, I see it all now. The picture is a tolerably convincing one, and you do appear to have been a lucky man to have survived for this long."

"I believe I have the beating of Vic Bales," Kelly said.

"And Taylor Vaughan?" the judge asked quizzically.

"That's a different class of man," Kelly admitted. "I don't see him as much of a fighter. I'd bet on his brains and breeding, but they don't count for much when there's blood flying."

"Don't underestimate Taylor Vaughan," Harrison Reed said seriously. "He was, at the end of the War between the States, one of the youngest colonels in the Union Army." The judge deliberately snapped his fingers in Kelly's face. "I'm still of the mind to dismiss your testimony against the gentleman. I have found him above reproach."

Kelly was convinced otherwise, but he said nothing, since he had no wish to get into a potentially damaging argument with Harrison Reed, who was at least tentatively on his side; so he merely smiled and raised his eyebrows in a questioning manner.

"Are you sure you want to go on with this, Kelly?" Harrison Reed demanded. "You've been severely wounded, and the risks you have to face can only get worse."

"When I put my hand to the plough,

146

Judge, I never turn back."

"Bravely said," Harrison Reed approved. "I have it within my power to appoint you a temporary deputy United States marshal. This would allow you complete freedom of movement, pay, expenses, and every help which the law can give its servants. At the end of this business, I would terminate your appointment without prejudice to any of the benefits earned."

"Sounds good," Kelly admitted. "Not that I've any qualifications, and I could turn out a real flop."

"You're no man's fool, Kelly," Harrison Reed said dismissively. "I wouldn't have come this far with you if I had believed you were. Normally, a man would need a long record as a successful law enforcer for acceptance as a deputy United States marshal, but I'm prepared to bend the rules here in the interests of us both. Even so I'd prefer it if my actions did not have to be too closely examined by the Department of Justice. So attempt nothing untoward."

"I'll keep it legal," Kelly promised, "and do my best for you. The kind of arrangement you propose will suit me fine."

"Good. I feel the end should justify the means."

"Then we have a deal."

The judge gave his chin a satisfied jerk. "I'll go through to my office and write out the necessary certificate of appointment. I'll find you a badge too. I cannot let you leave here without either." He smiled thinly. "I imagine you'll be heading for Renton at once?"

"That's where I'll be riding, sir."

"Do you wish to see Jean Troy before you leave?"

"I don't see the need," Kelly answered. "She's most likely still not feeling her best, and further talk would do her more harm than good. All I want for her is safety. I'm sure she'll be safe enough with you, Judge."

"Of course," Harrison Reed said, and left the room, his footfalls moving deeper into the claiming silence of the house.

Kelly listened as the man's movements ceased. After that he stepped up to the window and looked out at the lawn and its surrounding shrubs. For the next fifteen minutes he was required to exercise patience. Then the judge re-entered. Harrison Reed carried a piece of writing in one hand and a deputy U.S. marshal's shield in the other. He pinned the badge on Kelly's shirtfront; then gave him the certificate and said: "What happens next is mainly up to you. Good luck — Marshal."

"Thank you," Kelly said, putting the paper into a coat pocket.

"You may go, Kelly."

Kelly stood his ground.

"There was something else?"

"If Taylor Vaughan learns that I came to your house this morning and left with a badge on my chest, it must alert him to his danger from you."

"I suppose that is in prospect," the judge admitted. "Perhaps I'll ask him to dinner again and see how he behaves. The situation has its complications. But you must let me handle things here."

"There's no other way," Kelly agreed with finality.

The judge offered his hand. Kelly took it and they shook. After that Kelly left Harrison Reed's property and went again to the livery barn, where he claimed his horse. The animal, clearly well-rested and fed, seemed pleased to see him, and it wanted to be on its way the instant that he had led it clear of the barn and mounted up. So anxious was it to get going that he actually had to hold it down until they had crossed the town limits and were out upon the signposted trail to Renton. Now he let it run — until it had worked off its excess energy — and then he made himself comfortable above the steady knocking of its hooves and watched as the plains of central Wyoming came rolling at him again.

Noon arrived. The heat of the day greatly increased. Kelly found himself blowing a little and sleeving off a lot. He had a mere fifteen miles to travel, so he pressed on without a break, wondering where his enemies were at this time and how far their plans against Renton had developed since yesterday; yet, despite the ever-present risk of it — in view of Vic Bales's attempt to bushwhack him that morning — he had no real fear of attack just then, and it came as a surprise to him when he felt a shiver pass through his mount's withers and heard the brute emit a low snort of warning.

Startled back to total alertness, Kelly threw a glance across his right shoulder and at once perceived movement behind him. He tightened rein on his horse, determined not to let fear take over as yet, for he had strayed a little from the beaten way and been riding grass where cows were much in evidence. He could well be trespassing, and about to be pulled up by indignant cowboys, so he allowed the six riders that he could count galloping along in his wake to draw near enough for the main details of their faces and persons to become visible; but he repented this risky check on his progress as a gun banged and a bullet passed close enough to his right ear to be plainly audible.

Now he drove his spurs into his mount's flanks and, pulling his head down, turned into the west, for the only broken land in the vicinity appeared to lie in that direction. More shots came from the rear, but most of them missed him by a wide margin, and he made no attempt to return the firing. It was all ride, but he was not afraid of that. His horse was a good one, and his skills as a rider were higher than most. Though he had delayed his flight, he had gone to the gallop soon enough, and he had no doubt that he would outdistance his hunters quite easily when he reached terrain where deception and horsemanship would make all the difference. Everything depended on calmness and clear thinking, and he was as steady as a rock today.

But then fortune turned completely against him. He spurred on the upgrade towards a low ridge that seemed to extend for a mile or so across his path. Reaching the summit, he prepared to ride hell-for-leather down the reverse side, seeking to increase his lead; but now he saw a drop directly before him of about sixty feet into the waters of a lake and was forced to haul in with all his strength and heave his mount up and round to the right, cursing inwardly as the abruptly trembling horse started to lose its footing and slide sideways. Both he and it wrestled with gravity, and they overcame their danger and resumed travel along the summit of the ridge itself. But his hunters were still there, and had swung out to form a line of six guns across which he must now run the gauntlet.

From the corner of his right eye Kelly saw gunsmoke fluffing. A bullet raked the front of his saddle, and another burned his right sleeve. He spurred on resolutely, but his confidence began to drain away for all that. He knew he wasn't going to make it. Then, braced to absorb lead himself, he heard the sullen whack of a slug entering his mount's barrel. The horse buckled sideways, neighing in despair, and next moment it rolled off the edge of the land crest and man and beast separated and both pitched into space.

Now they were plunging, and it seemed to Kelly that they described a figure of eight about each other. The sky-stained waters of the lake rushed up to meet them, and suddenly the shadowy tomb that awaited them in the depths was revealed.

7

KELLY hit the surface of the lake back first. It was a warm day, and the chase had caused him to sweat profusely, but his immersion — in liquid still chilled by meltwaters — numbed him instantly to the heart, and he sank into the depths without any hope of checking himself. Down Kelly went, settling like a rock statue, and the sunlight was dimming to a honey shade around him when his soles finally touched bottom and he hung amidst black boulders and silvery sand, air bubbling from the corners of his mouth and the icy paralysis still holding him in thrall.

His lungs were almost empty as he stared upwards through the purifying bands of transparency between him and the sky. He feared drowning now as moments ago he had feared a bullet.

He seemed anchored to the floor of the lake, but got himself started upwards somehow, and rose slowly after that, angling to his right above the bottom like some wraith of the charnel house. He estimated that he'd just about make it back to the air before his lungs gave out completely; but then he was afflicted by another sudden change of luck as his ankles became entrapped in weed and he found himself held fast in an area of shadow beyond which he could just make out the split and broken stone along the foot of the lake's northern wall.

Kelly's suffering now beggared all description, and worst of all he found himself suffering from moments of memory loss which came and went erratically. He realized that he was no longer capable of coherent thought and fully coordinated movements. Forced to it, he let instinct take over and, doubling like an eel, grabbed the weed near its union with the lake floor and yanked frantically, pulling it out by the roots. Now he found himself free again and once more started to drift upwards — his progress as abnormal as previously; and then, in a split second of mental clarity, he perceived that his recent drift to the right had not been due so much to a lack of physical buoyancy as the presence of a current which was again holding down his body and forcing it sideways rather than up.

Literally at his last gasp, he floated right up to the northern wall of the lake, his crown jarring against the rock there and, short of the normal rebound from such a meeting, his skull slipped into one of the breaks in the formation which he had earlier glimpsed and a continuation of the movement raised his face upwards into a chimney-like slot within the stone wall where his straining nose and mouth just cleared the water which had been drowning him and caused him to obey his instinctive impulse and attempt breathing.

Air rushed into Kelly's lungs. He

luxuriated in the renewal of his heart action and the cleansing of his blood. His brain cleared too, and he soon realized that his face had entered a source of air which had been around for ages, since this was plainly no pocket but a continuous supply of the freshest and purest air from the atmosphere above the lake and suggested that he was lying at the bottom of a fissure which travelled upwards to join some eroded duct from the outer world.

Whatever the exact truth of that might be, he knew himself safe for as long as he wished to remain in this state of suspension. Yet that was the slowly dawning horror of it. For he lay thus physically distorted in a natural trap which was gradually freezing him back into the state of semi-paralysis that had seized him after he had first become submerged in the depths of the lake. Safe he might be in a sense, but if he didn't soon do something rather drastic to help himself again, his face was going to settle back below the waterline as his numbness increased and he would then suffer the fate of drowning which he had by an incredible trick of chance lately managed to avoid.

Clearly his sole aim now must be to get back to the surface, but his seeming good fortune still made him hang back. For if he drew a deep breath and wriggled out of the rift which contained the life-giving flow of air, he would be in every sense back at the bottom of the lake again and wholly dependent on what oxygen that single inhalation brought him. Once clear of this spot, he would have little hope of finding it a second time — if things again went completely wrong — before his air gave out and drowning once more became inevitable. He was convinced that there was a jungle of weed out there that he had not yet encountered and that the current which had lately interfered with his return to the surface was strong enough to make him its prisoner and give him another bad time when he met it again. Thus the temptation to hang on in his present little haven until his limbs stiffened and escape became physically impossible was almost more than he could resist.

But he was no quitter, and the force of his will remained to him. He must withdraw from the bottom of the fissure this very moment; if he didn't it would be too late. So, filling his chest to the limit, he shut his eyes and settled downwards, floating out of the rift's base, and after that he raised his hands prayerfully above his head and kicked upwards with all the strength he could find, forgetting all that could go wrong and only concentrating on all that should go right.

He travelled upwards unimpeded. Neither the weed nor the current troubled him now, and he wondered in what degree these fearsome impediments had been barriers of the mind as he broke surface and floated there, treading water. Then, accepting that even now he was far from being out of trouble, he looked above and about him, wondering whether the enemies who had brought him to this pass were still in the vicinity and keeping watch.

Kelly could see nobody atop the cliff that overlooked him. How long had he been under? Three or four minutes? Yes, at least that, and possibly longer. Long enough, anyway, for the average man to have drowned thrice over. It was unlikely that the villains who had brought about his fall were still watching the lake. True, he couldn't see its banks too well from here, but it seemed a reasonable supposition that the badmen had left the area believing him dead.

He started to swim for the western shore. By now he was feeling half exhausted and the bank appeared miles beyond him. He supposed it was in fact about four hundred yards, but swimming was an exercise with which he was not too familiar, and the threshing of his limbs was already beginning to weigh him down. It would be easy to settle and choke before he even realized that he was sinking, but he could only bear up and go on until he could go no more.

So he forgot about the shore and simply swam. Changing his strokes at frequent intervals, he made about the same progress with his dog-paddle as he did the crawl. Before long it seemed as if he had spent his entire life swimming, and that this cold lake was his world. Often he lay back and trod water, spitting and gasping rather desperately, and he was close to giving up and allowing himself to sink like a stone, when he heard a pair of young male voices yelling at him to hold on. He did just that and, raising himself high enough in the water, saw two swimmers making for him with the speed and grace of experts. Right then he didn't envy them their skill and, when they reached him, was content just to lie on his back and let them support him to the shore, where one of them turned him onto his face amidst the silver grit and pebbles and began to pump him out rather vigorously. "I'm okay!" Kelly gasped, tipping over and balancing on his hands. "If you want to finish me off, mister, that's the best way to go about it!"

"There's gratitude for you!" the youthful rescusitator said to his companion.

"We can always throw him back!" the second young man pointed out. "Who's to know the difference? He don't look worth much anyhow!"

"You boys done?" Kelly asked sourly, sitting there and dripping like a waterlogged hound. "You might show some respect for a poor unfortunate."

"Will you look there?" the first young man pleaded. "If we ain't gone and rescued a U.S. deputy. The badge is nigh as big as he is. No wonder the cowson couldn't swim with all that metal on him."

"And who are you two smart asses?" Kelly asked rudely. "Billy the Kid and sidekick?"

"Naw, just a couple of working men," he was informed. "We're part of a party herdin' over yonder. Brad Cullins, the foreman, ordered us this way to find out what all the blamed shootin' was about."

"Thank you, Mr Cullins!" Kelly said, gazing upwards with pious eyes.

"How about thank you Mr Trench and Mr Dobbs?"

Kelly lowered his eyes and considered the pair with a faintly jaundiced expression on his face. Both were long-limbed and merry-eyed, with lean, healthy faces, but one had black hair and the other a thatch so pale that it was almost white. "Thank you Mr Trench and Mr Dobbs. So which is which?"

"I'm Dobbs," said the young man with the pale hair.

"That means you're Trench," Kelly said to the dark one.

"Fair takes your breath away, don't he, Harry?" Trench observed. "He worked that out all by himself." He

164

grinned, his mouth becoming wide and toothy. "Yeah, I'm Trench — or was this morning when I got kicked out of bed. The foreman's called me something else a time or two since. But that ain't nothing new."

Kelly chuckled understandingly. "Thanks, boys," he said sincerely. "I'd have been a goner if you hadn't fished me out."

"You're welcome, Marshal," Dobbs returned, grinning negligently. "Helped make a change." He squeezed at the wet garments that were clinging to his flesh. "Did you ever go herding cows?"

"Sure," Kelly said.

"Talk about crime and punishment!"

"It's a chore," Kelly conceded — "and that's a fact."

"What happened to you, Marshal?" Trench asked curiously. "We rode up in time to see you swimming. Nothing more."

"I was set on by a guy named Vic Bales and the skunks who ride with him," Kelly explained. "They were shooting at me, and I was running — and I came slap-bang, all of a sudden, over the ridge that overlooks the lake. I swung my horse westwards, and he caught a pill in the ribs. Over we both went, splash into the water. It was touch-and-go there, because I got held down awhile, but I made it off the bottom and it figures that Bales and his scum think I've cashed in. My horse has gone where all the good horses go, and he won't be coming back. But I'm sure as the devil going to get where I've got to go."

"Where's that?" the blond Dobbs inquired.

"Renton."

"Not much there, Marshal," Dobbs sighed. "The whisky's bad, the men are idiots, and the women have been plumb worn out by the Cavalry."

"Common tale for these parts," Kelly remarked dryly. "Thank God it's a warm day. I'd hate to be wearing these wet things if it wasn't."

"Tell us some more about this here Bales guy and his bunch," Dobbs invited. "Sounds exciting."

"Forget that!" Kelly snorted. "It's enough to say Renton's due to be raided by Bales and company. He had only about half his men with him just now, so the devilry's near."

"All funnin' aside," Dobbs said anxiously, "my ma lives in Renton."

"Heck, boy!" Kelly exclaimed. "I'm not happy about that!"

"Oh, it's true enough, Marshal," Trench said rather unnecessarily. "His mother does live in Renton. Harry always tells the truth once a day. But only because he runs out of lies."

"That sidewinder didn't have a ma," Dobbs commented. "He sprung up under a rotten tree — among all the other toadstools!"

"Ha, ha!" Trench sniffed. "If you need anybody to help protect that corker's ma, Marshal, you don't need to look beyond me. She only did the world one bad turn!"

"Boys," Kelly said deliberately, "I need all the help I can get. And I tell you both, you've already done the lady in question a fair hand's turn by pulling me out of the lake. If you want to do her another, get me to that man Cullins."

"Good as done," Dobbs said, pointing to the grass beyond the raw, flood-shaped earth which formed a low wall around the lake's perimeter. "Our hosses are waiting over there."

"Capital!"

"Can you stand up, Marshal?"

"Yes, Harry, and walk too," Kelly responded, forcing himself erect and then bracing his legs. "Let's go to your horses. I'll ride with which of you it suits best."

"Well, he ain't what you'd call safe," Dobbs said provocatively, jerking a thumb at his pal, "so you'd better ride with me."

"Only make your Will first," Trench retaliated.

They climbed away from the shore.

After that Kelly trudged unsteadily across the grass between the two younger men, and they came soon enough to where two solid-coloured range ponies were standing with their heads down and reins trailing. While Trench mounted the smaller horse, Dobbs climbed on the larger one and, offering an arm, helped Kelly up behind him. Then, with Trench surging into the lead, they moved off across the prairie, heading south-westwards, and after a minute or two they came in sight of a particularly lush portion of the grass where a party of cowboys had a fire burning and were branding the many calves from a big herd of white-faced Hereford cattle.

As the mounts bearing Kelly and his two young saviours neared the work area, a horseman suddenly broke away from the figures close to the branding bed and began galloping towards the newcomers. Hard-bitten of face and deep of chest, this man had real muscles and a look of natural authority about him, and Kelly didn't imagine that he would be far wrong in supposing the other to be the foreman who had been mentioned earlier. "Mr Cullins?" he called.

"Yeah, I'm Brad Cullins!" the other shouted back, halting his strawberry gelding in the path of the two oncoming horses and forcing their riders to draw rein also. "Who are you, mister?"

"Sam Kelly — riding marshal."

"Me and Harry fished him out of the lake," Trench said.

"You look a nice pair of drowned rats all right," the foreman commented scathingly, though his attention was more on Kelly than anybody as he spoke. "How the dickens did you get in there, Marshal? Had you dived in for a swim?"

"Hell, no!" Kelly answered. "I've always held that cleanliness is next to godliness, but I wouldn't say I was that keen personally on water in large amounts."

"He got set on by badmen," Dobbs

said helpfully, if a sight too cheerfully.

And Kelly swiftly told the part of his story that mattered over again, uttering it much as he had done to his rescuers.

Cullins rasped his chin, grimacing. "If you aren't about as welcome as a yellowjacket at a picnic, Marshal Kelly! What am I to do with you?"

"Take me to your boss," Kelly said. "I've an important job to do, and I need his help. It would not please my boss, Judge Harrison Reed of South Hills, if you turned me away."

"Oh, him!" Cullins said indifferently. "The second son of God, wouldn't you say?"

"Big man when he holds court, Mr Cullins," Kelly allowed diplomatically.

"He's that," Cullins sighed, pointing at Dobbs. "Get off that cayuse, Harry! Let the marshal have it. Help yourself to another mount from among the spares yonder." He gave his attention to Trench now. "Get back to work, Abe!"

"Now that ain't right!" Trench declared aggrievedly. "Don't Harry and me get the chance to change our sodden clothing?"

"Got a change of duds with you?"

"No, sir, be damned if I have!"

"The boss will skin me alive," Cullins said, "if I let you two go back to the bunkhouse before the working day is over. It's your own faults, you lazy good-for-nothings!"

Dobbs, who had lately dismounted, began to cough in a frightful manner.

"Now, Brad," Trench pleaded, "you and Mr Sizeland know all about poor Harry's weak chest!"

"What a fellow has to put up with on the Bar S ranch!" Cullins complained bitterly. "I know I'm a sinner, but what did I ever do to wind up with a pair like you? Your dear friend, Abe, will be littering up this earth long after they've run out of timber to bury the last of his generation." The foreman carefully spat out his bile. "I suppose I've got to risk proving once again that I'm not one of Simon Legree's bastards. Go and find yourself that horse, Dobbs. Then you and Abe can ride back to the bunkhouse and change. And if you two grinning monkeys waste a minute more than's necessary — " He gave up at that point, obviously lost for words, and waved dismissively; and Trench and Dobbs — the one riding and the other running after him — went on their way rejoicing.

"We shan't get any more work out of them today," Cullins said, grinning covertly at Kelly.

"They that bad?" Kelly asked, having eased forward into the saddle which the ash blond young man had vacated a minute or so before.

"Pests!" Cullins chuckled. "Otherwise the life and soul of the ranch — but they mustn't be allowed to know it."

"Reckon not," Kelly agreed, smiling. "They saved my life sure enough. Or would they have done as much for a dog?"

"Especially for a dog," Cullins replied.

"Come on, Marshal! Or you're likely to be the next fellow with a bad chest!"

Getting the feel of the horse under him, Kelly started following the foreman westwards across the range. No further word was spoken, and it was about fifteen minutes later when they crossed a ridge clad in live oak and made their way down the other side on to a worn flat where a red-timbered ranch house had been built amidst a spread of cattle pens, horse corrals, and a variety of outbuildings, the whole reaching back towards higher ground and the dark glory of a westering sun haloed by purple cumulus. The wind, on the shift and rising, put a tremor in both the grass and the new leaf behind the descending riders.

Into the ranch yard they loped, and drew rein at the hitching rail near the kitchen door. Answering the glint of expectancy which Kelly saw in the foreman's eye, a window flew up and a skinny mophead of a woman looked out, all gimlet eyes and arms too pale and wiry to dwell upon. "What do you want, Brad Cullins?" she demanded. "It ain't nothing like six o'clock yet!"

"Needs must, Lucy," the foreman assured her comfortably. "Is the boss there?"

"In the parlour."

"Kindly fetch him."

"He's got Arnie Grigson with him."

"I've got a deputy United States marshal with me."

"That?" the woman said, squinting hard at Kelly and clearly unimpressed. "Huh, the law ain't what I'd call fussy these days!"

"Just ask the boss if he'll come out here and see me," Cullins urged none too patiently.

The peculiar little woman banged the window shut, then left the glass and moved back into the house beyond.

"Where does she hail from?" Kelly asked, shivering as cold airs from the rainy quarter blustered around his wet person.

"That's Lucy Hume," the foreman

said. "She's touched in the head. Pay her no heed."

Kelly grinned wryly to himself. Lucy Hume might be touched in the head, but the plain truth did not escape her. He could see from his reflection in one of the windowpanes that he was at present no specimen of which the law might be proud.

A minute went by. Then the back door opened suddenly, and through it stepped a square-shouldered, balding man, with a piece of cake in one hand and an open book in the other. He wore garments of the highest quality, but his waistcoat hung loose about his middle and the flaps of his cord breeches were only partially buttoned. Though most probably a man of superior mind, the other looked just untidy enough to make Kelly feel better about his own appearance; and he lifted a hand in salute as the newcomer nodded at him and said: "Good afternoon."

"This is Marshal Kelly, Mr Sizeland," Brad Cullins introduced. "He's been in the wars — and got a rare old story to tell. It seems Renton is due to be attacked."

"Hey?" Sizeland inquired, looking Kelly up and down now and tut-tutting.

"By a gang," Kelly explained, "that sends in men dressed as Indians to draw off a town's fighting men before sending others in as white raiders to strip the place."

"That's novel, by damn!" Sizeland commented, spitting crumbs as he ate a mouthful of his cake. "You're shivering, man! You'll catch your death!"

"I was hoping you'd help me to a change of clothing and a horse," Kelly said. "I've been to the bottom of a lake, and my mount is dead."

"I see."

"He's Judge Harrison Reed's man," Cullins put in significantly.

"Mustn't offend him," Sizeland said shortly. "I'll be glad to provide a horse and a change of clothing, Marshal."

"I've more to tell, Mr Sizeland," Kelly advised.

"Tell it when you're dry," the rancher said. "Climb down and follow me." Then he looked at his foreman. "There's coffee on the kitchen hob, Cullins. You and Grigson can help yourselves while you're waiting for me to rejoin you. We have some talking of our own to do."

Sizeland faced round. He re-entered the ranch house, and Kelly pursued him through the warmth of the kitchen and into the hall beyond. From there he was conducted up an enclosed stairwell, along an upper passage, and into a small bedroom at the rear of the dwelling. Leaving him there, the cattleman said: "Get those wet things off, Marshal. I'll bring you a dry rig-out. I've plenty of old clothing, and shan't expect you to return the stuff. I'll be back in a minute."

Kelly stripped himself to the buff, and Sizeland made the swift return he had promised. Besides a pile of

178

clothing and a pair of boots, he brought a thick towel. This he tossed to the naked lawman. "Dry yourself off," he ordered, "then put this lot on. When you've done it, come downstairs. You'll find me in the kitchen with Cullins and Grigson."

"Got you," Kelly said, as the rancher went out again. "I'll be down as quickly as I can."

Listening to Sizeland's descent through the enclosed stairway, Kelly dried himself off, then put on the clothing that had been fetched in to him, stamping on the boots when he felt otherwise presentable. Finally he picked up his gunbelt from the dresser on which he had earlier placed it and freed his still firmly holstered pistol from its safety string. A quick examination showed the weapon to be in good order, though he doubted that the cartridges in its cylinder — or those in the loops of his belt for the matter of that — would fire after their long immersion in water; but there was nothing he could do about that for the minute — except hope that Sizeland would be prepared to replace his suspect ammunition with some that could be fully trusted — so he swung the gunbelt back around his waist and latched it fast.

After walking downstairs, Kelly went through into the kitchen. He saw Sizeland sitting in a wooden armchair beside the cooking range and looking pensive. Brad Cullins was stroking a bushy brow nearby, while a large, fattening man — Grigson presumably — was bowed off the mantelpiece, eyes gazing down into the hearth between his bent arms, and he alone gave any recognition of Kelly's entry by shifting his chin a little to the left. "Gentlemen," the newly made lawman prompted.

Sizeland stirred and glanced round at him, smiling thinly when he saw that his cast-offs fitted Kelly about adequately. But he made no allusion to the fact as he said: "I believe this is going to interest you, Marshal.

Anyhow, I'd like to see how far your mind follows my own."

"Well?" Kelly inquired curiously.

"I've been listening to what I imagine to be the rest of your story from Brad Cullins," the rancher began, pausing expectantly.

"Okay," Kelly said. "He knows it."

"Well," Sizeland resumed, "just before you and Brad got here, Arnie Grigson had come riding in from my west range. Arnie spends most of his time working from a line shack out there. It's high and hidden, and there's a trail not far in front of it, so he often sees travellers go by. Today he saw a bunch of riders go through, but had the feeling that these men turned off to the left not far beyond his hiding place onto the path that leads to an old mine in a place of rock and little else.

"Grigson's first thought was rustlers, Marshal, and that's what brought him to the ranch house. He could still be right, of course, but I'm not too worried about it because most of the

181

graze west of here is being given a rest and I only keep a small herd of ageing cows in that area." The rancher gave Kelly a narrow and faintly questioning glance at this juncture. "Assuming I've heard your story right, Marshal, I have the suspicion that those riders Grigson saw could be even more dangerous visitors than he imagined. What do you think about that?"

Pulling a serious face, Kelly prepared to tell him.

8

"I DON'T think there's any chance," Kelly said, "that the men Grigson saw were the ones who attacked me. Apart from the direction being wrong, it's unlikely they could have ridden as far as you suggest in the time. As you've been clearly hinting, Mr Sizeland, the probability is that those guys Grigson spotted are the other half of Vic Bales's gang. Strikes me — knowing a mite about their habits — they intend to use the old mine you mentioned as a start-off point for their raid on Renton."

"My thought exactly," Sizeland said. "Good. We'll take action at once."

"You want to help with the dangerous part?" Kelly stressed.

"If there's a threat to Renton developing near my place," the rancher returned, "I'm duty bound to turn out against it. Correct?"

"There's no compulsion present," Kelly advised.

"And none felt," Sizeland assured him — "outside the fact. A man best serves others when first he serves himself, Marshal. Renton is my base of supply. There are folk there that I rate as friends and have need of. Any disruption in Renton would harm my Bar S, and I allow nothing to harm the Bar S that I can prevent."

"That's natural," Kelly said.

"Then let's get to it," Sizeland said briskly, rising in the same manner. "Go and saddle my horse, Arnie. Brad — you round up the men we've got immediately available. Every manjack now — because strength does usually lie in numbers."

Cullins and Grigson immediately walked out of the house to do their employer's bidding. That left Kelly standing just into the kitchen from the hall doorway. Sizeland shot him a glance of inquiry.

"I'll need the continued use of the horse on which I rode in," Kelly said, "and I'd be obliged for a box of forty-four ammunition. I figure most of the cartridges in my gun and belt are too wet to fire now."

The cattleman jerked his chin curtly, then rounded Kelly and passed towards the main rooms of the dwelling's ground floor. He returned shortly with a box of a dozen shells in either hand and gave them to the marshal. "That should keep you going for a while," he observed. "Pray God it doesn't come to that much shooting!"

"Amen," Kelly agreed, breaking out the contents of the boxes and putting them into his trouser-pockets. "Thanks."

"Got a plan?" Sizeland asked.

"Mainly wait and see," Kelly confessed. "You're the man who knows the country. I won't argue with your lead for now, sir."

Arnie Grigson put his sad and crumpled face in at the kitchen door then and said: "Your horse is ready for you, boss, and the foreman's found up four guys to go with us. That makes eight of us."

"I can count, Arnie," Sizeland said. "Who are the men?"

"'Turkey' Bronson, Phil Jordan — and those two."

A pained expression came to the cattleman's face. "Trench and Dobbs?"

"Brad told you they were soaked after pulling the marshal out of the lake," Grigson reminded. "He had to let them come on in and change their duds."

Sizeland gestured resignedly. "We haven't so much scraped the bottom of the barrel as gone through it."

"With any luck, boss, that pair could get shot," Grigson said hopefully.

"Not a chance," Sizeland returned, grinning bleakly. "In my lengthening experience, the devil does look after his own, and those two boys must be under his special protection." He headed for the back door and the ranch yard beyond it. "Come on, Marshal!

Let's get on with it! It'll either be dark or raining before we know it. Maybe both."

Kelly followed the rancher outside. The impromptu gathering which Grigson had told of was at the middle of the yard. Brad Cullins sat his mount at the forefront, and he held a blue roan stallion by its reins. As Kelly went to the horse that had been accepted as his to use for now, he saw Abe Trench and Harry Dobbs lounging in their saddles behind two older men of stalwart appearance who were undoubtedly Phil Jordan and 'Turkey' Bronson. Trench and Dobbs were smoking cigarettes and looking distinctly sorry for themselves. As he smiled inwardly, Kelly was sure that the youthful duo would now be happy to herd cattle in their wet clothing. Trench's insistence on their moral right to get their sodden things off had not worked out at all well for them.

Kelly mounted up. Rancher Sizeland walked to the blue roan stallion and did the same. Then the cattleman raised an arm and pointed westwards, and the company spurred into motion, hitting a fast trot straightaway. Sizeland surged ahead, and all present — including Kelly — rode along in his wake. The party quickly left the ranch yard behind, following the base of the ridge which Kelly and Brad Cullins had recently crossed to reach the Bar S ranch house.

The weather, so good earlier, was now swiftly going to pieces. Dark cloud was streaming up from the south-west, and it seemed likely all present were going to get wet. Kelly heard Arnie Grigson curse what appeared to be coming, and he was forced to admit to himself that he had no love of riding in the rain; but there were things that had to be done regardless of the weather, and the tackling of the badmen who could have gone into hiding nearby was the first and least of them.

Presently the plain ahead elongated to fit the base of an irregular formation of grassy benches and outcropping ridges of granite. Many of these minor heights carried small stands of timber, while over to the right and prominent upon the northern scene, a cluster of crags, grey and jagged, stood out of the gathering murk. Now droplets of water flew among the riders, and the wind droned. Breasting into the threatening airs, the men set their horses climbing, and Sizeland angled away from the weather quarter and led the ranch party through clumps of pine scrub and ranks of aspen, soon bringing his followers to a trail which appeared to cross the highest parts of the immediate country on its way northwards.

As Kelly judged would be the case on meeting the beaten way, Sizeland now made a sharp turn to the right. The rancher led on for another quarter of a mile, then fetched left onto the ground which, through its deep scrape-marks and indentations, showed that it had once been cleared of its smaller rocks and such to provide access to the iron-tyred vehicles whose ruts were still faintly visible in the road which they had impressed for themselves.

The horsemen pursued the old waggon road on a course that was slightly upgrade. They passed through one or two thickets of blackthorn and mountain ash en route, but the path remained mostly bare and rocky, and they arrived very soon on the ground where the crags seen from back on the grass began. Here the road entered a steepwalled and narrow cutting — which would have no more than admitted a waggon — and the riders were starting to pack together, when there was an uproar from a thicket about thirty yards behind them and a horseman suddenly erupted into full view, fighting down a frightened mount. Craning abruptly, Kelly watched the battle between man and horse during the seconds that it lasted; then, as the rider won out, saw man and beast go diving for the trail north which the people from the Bar S had so recently left.

Well forward in Sizeland's bunched up party, Kelly had to suppress his impatience with the horsemen about him and allow them to turn their mounts as best they could manage according to their gifts; and, by the time he could jink clear of the reversing animals and put their swearing owners behind him, the fugitive was far down the shallow slope up which the ranch party had just come and in a fair way to riding clear.

Kelly went after the fellow just the same, yelling back across his shoulder: "Put some life into it, you guys! I want that man — and I want him alive!"

"You heard the marshal!" Sizeland roared. "Open out — open out!"

Voices raised in the spirit of high sport, the dark-haired Trench and Dobbs, his blond pal, went rocketing past the lawman, ready to make a race of it; but this had hardly occurred when Dobbs let out a howl of fright as his horse abruptly caught back in its stride and reared almost to the vertical, shooting him out of his seat as it twisted away from a king rattlesnake which had just appeared in its path and was now spitting venomously and coiled in readiness to strike.

Kelly heaved in, barely avoiding the fallen Dobbs and bumped by the cowboy's settling horse, while Trench — whose mount had also been frightened by the big snake — went spilling in the opposite direction and thus added to the chaos in front of the other riders. Meantime, the rattler, no longer closely threatened, went slithering away into the rocks and soon disappeared, leaving Kelly to bite his tongue once more and reflect that the snake's presence had doubtless been the cause of frightening out the hidden horseman in the first place and providing the start to this fiasco.

"Consarned snake!" Dobbs bawled, jumping up and doing something that resembled a war dance. "I've done busted my butt!"

"What the hell's that?" Trench demanded aggrievedly, holding his crotch. "Blasted saddle! No woman'll want me now! I'm done for life!"

"No woman would have had you anyhow!" Cullins, the foreman, snarled heartlessly. "Get out of the way, you stupid noodles! The horses have got more sense than you have!"

The two young men limped out of the road, one going to the left and the other to the right; and, with the way cleared, Kelly and the other men still in their saddles spurred forward again, resuming their gallop towards the trail to the east of them.

They arrived at the track about a minute later. Kelly was well to the fore now. He yanked left on the logic of the situation and began heading northwards; but he saw almost at once that the trail was empty before him and soon raised a staying hand. There was little point running the horses flat when even their quarry's direction could not be ascertained on the undisturbed land before them. Plainly, the ranch party's enforced delay back there had created the vital difference and given the fugitive ample time to make good his escape. It simply could not be helped, and was yet another vexation to assimilate. "Dammit!" he said weakly, glancing at Sizeland, who had just reined in beside him. "So what d'you reckon?"

"No sense going on," the rancher affirmed. "He's given us the slip."

"What's it to be now?"

"The same as before, I suppose," Sizeland responded. "We were going to the old Ablett diggings. Has it occurred to you, Marshal, that the rest of those villains could have been at the mine? The fellow who bolted up there could have been their look-out and saw the chance to draw us off."

"Don't fancy it," Kelly said, starting to turn his horse. "It was that snake started him running."

"I'll take you to the mine," Sizeland said, fetching his mount about likewise.

"That way we'll cover our first intention and see anything that's there to be seen," Kelly acknowledged, surging after his companion as the cattleman passed through the presently turning riders who had been at their backs and resumed leading from the front.

Riding back, they swung again at the turn-off, repeating their shallow climb to the cutting where matters had previously gone wrong. This time nothing happened to interfere with their progress and, exercising due caution, they passed between the narrow walls and emerged in a rectangular space of not great dimensions which, like the waggon road, had clearly been improved by the work of human hands. There was a rockface to the right of the oblong, and an entrance was visible at the foot of the stone. Just inside this hole — which was clearly the way into the Ablett mine — a heap of broken tools, household utensils, and worn out clothing lay gathering rust and mildew. There was a faint smell of fresh horse urine in the air, but seemed to be nobody around, and Sizeland said: "This place used up Paul Ablett's life, Marshal, and not more than eating money did he ever take out of it."

"It was the death of him, you mean?"

"The doctor called it dust on the lung," the rancher answered, nodding. "Paul has been dead these twelve years. He was my best friend, and believed to the last that this rock up here had a heart of gold. If only he had come into cattle with me; but there was a woman between us — and she was a worthless hussy."

"Sad story," Kelly commented and, stepping down and passing about his mount's rear, entered the mine, conscious at once of new mineral odours in the air and shapeless objects lying against the walls of the entrance tunnel at the point where the daylight began failing before the excavation's inner darkness. "Have you got a match?"

Sizeland walked up to join him. The rancher struck a match on the wall of the tunnel and held up the flame. Light spilled and flickered around the stuttering fire, and Kelly was able to bend and examine the objects lying against the bottom of the walls on either hand. Picking up the nearest one and prying inside it, he found that he was holding no more than a webbing pack which had been hastily stuffed with a man's riding garments. Grunting, Kelly handed the pack to Sizeland, then picked up another like it and perceived that it was wadded in the same fashion. A third pack was crammed with a similar filling, and no doubt the same went for two others lying nearby. The match went out just then, but Sizeland soon lighted another, and they moved a few steps deeper into the mine, coming to the first of its work galleries. Here they kicked against two rows of riding boots and then halted before a large, flat-topped stone which was covered with dishes holding various paints and ochres that gave off the mineral odour which Kelly had detected in the atmosphere on first entering the mine shaft.

He needed to see no more, for he was now certain that the half of Vic Bales's followers who took the part of the renegade Indians had entered these diggings recently and made a quick change to their savage identities, leaving again — probably within the last hour — to stir up trouble in Renton and thus pave the way for a swift raid by their unadorned colleagues who were undoubtedly poised outside the town by this time and just waiting for the signal to go.

"Does this mean what I think it means?" Sizeland asked, striking a third match as Kelly went round the containers of colouring matter and stirred each in turn with a sliver of wood, holding up a sample of each concoction to the light.

"You bet it does," Kelly said. "There's hurry stamped all over this. Renton is going to be raided this evening. Maybe those badmen are bent on getting this job over as quickly as they can."

"That could be it," Sizeland responded. "How far are we from Renton?"

"Three miles."

"A fifteen minute ride," Kelly calculated. "The man who escaped us just now would have been the one left to guard things here. He could be with his painted comrades and have told them what's happened by now."

"Any chance those villains will do what appears the sensible thing and run for it?" the rancher asked.

"Why should they?" Kelly asked. "The half of the gang that was here can't know about me and my place in things today. The probability is, those fellows will put their discovery here down to bad luck and figure it as your man Grigson did first off."

"That I have them pegged for rustlers or some such?"

"Exactly."

"They do appear at liberty to go ahead as planned," Sizeland acknowledged. "Nor would I suggest that you don't know your own business best. But can you be sure that the men who were here know nothing of your identity or movements today, Marshal? You could be taking a little for granted."

"I don't see where," Kelly said. "You can stretch doubt too far. Guessing at the routes which the two halves of the gang have travelled today, I don't see how they could have had contact since they separated. That means their lookout couldn't possibly have recognized me, and they can't have any idea that we'll be after them right away."

"Are we strong enough?"

"Only in terms of surprise, Mr Sizeland."

"I've got another two dozen men back on the ranch, Marshal," Sizeland tempted.

"No time to gather them," Kelly replied, shaking his head. "We'd get to Renton after dark and find the raid over."

"We'd better head for Renton right now — and just mind what we're doing."

"My sentiments exactly, Mr Sizeland," Kelly said. "Yes, we'll take care."

Kelly and the rancher turned away from the evidence of guilt which the renegades had left behind them. They walked out of the mine and into the thin rain that was falling now. The waiting Cullins and his five subordinates — still perched on their mounts — had bowed their faces and were studying their saddles, men become suitably stoical, and their boss looked up at them and said: "We're going to Renton, men. We've found signs in the mine which suggest the town will be raided this evening. Keep your eyes lifting. There'll probably be fighting at some stage."

Shrugging, Cullins looked around him, eyes daring any cowboy to pass a remark. Dobbs was afflicted by a spasm of raucous coughing, but nobody took much notice of that. Then Kelly and Sizeland remounted, and the rancher led round to the left and back into the cutting. Through it they passed and, out beyond the narrows, Sizeland called for a trot.

The party soon regained the trail and began heading north. They galloped now with the fine rain upon their backs, and the going was not too unpleasant. After covering about two miles, Sizeland yanked into a left turn and led his followers across the combers of some high meadowland, arriving at a wide, tree-clad mound where the trail pitched its descent through a rift which appeared to have carried water in the far past. Kelly assumed that Sizeland was going to stay with the track, and he had to make a hurried adjustment to his reins when the rancher went slanting off to the left just short of the rift's head and rode into the trees next to it, jinking onwards through the pines and undergrowth until the foliage broke and a drop appeared before them.

Sizeland raised a staying hand, and Kelly and the rest of the riders reined to a stop. They were near the edge of a cliff which overlooked a considerable bluff-walled formation of partially developed valleys that contained, in the first and nearest instance, a drab township that had no look of permanency about it and, in the ones that came after it, field, forest, lake and barren corners, the whole bursting at last upon the leaden west through a pass into which mighty prows of ribbed and discoloured rock advanced their frowning masses.

Kelly kneed his mount up to Sizeland's right elbow. "That's Renton down there?" he asked, jerking his chin at the rooftops almost immediately below.

"That's Renton," the cattleman answered. "And do you see what I see?"

Yes, Kelly had seen. Below them — and from the base of the rift which the ranch party had just avoided — a party of 'Indians' had just galloped into view, bows bent and fire arrows at the ready. Now, yelling savagely, the horsemen, resplendent in their warpaint and eagle feathers, loosed off their blazing shafts and rode on as the oil-doused cotton waste at the tops of the missiles followed the arrowheads to rest in the wooden walls of the main street and threatened a conflagration. This was, of course, a nuisance gesture designed to draw the attention of the startled townsfolk, since the galloping 'redmen' could not, for want of more fire, follow up on the first volley of arrows with another or subsequent ones, and the renegades simply slung their bows across their backs and began shooting with rifles instead, their main targets the windows of the stores and houses adjacent to their path.

"All right!" Kelly shouted, climbing his horse round as the popping of guns and tinkling of glass echoed up to the clifftop. "You've seen it, men!

Let's get down there and put an end to it!"

He gave the lead back through the trees, and spared nobody, least of all himself.

9

AS he emerged from the trees and headed into the rift which carried the trail down towards Renton, Kelly was aware of the owner of the Bar S drawing level with him, and he heard Sizeland shout: "Are you sure you know what you're doing, Marshal?"

Kelly knew what the man was driving at, but merely turned his head and gave a confident nod.

"The second party won't ride in if the first is attacked by us, dammit!" the rancher insisted.

This was no time to argue it, and Kelly didn't try. He simply turned his face to the front and steadied his horse into the descent, admitting to himself that the action which he had initiated here was something of a gamble. No matter how these doings were handled, half the enemy could escape — either as the 'redmen' fleeing after the first charge or as the white raiders withdrawing from the area before an actual assault was made — but, relying on the fact that the two parties were working as one — and that men usually stuck together in such circumstances — there was a good chance that, on realizing that their 'redskin' comrades were under attack, the waiting raiders would themselves gallop into town with guns blazing and thus place the entire gang in jeopardy. Much could indeed happen to invalidate that reasoning, and a number of variations on the situation could arise, but Kelly felt it just about worth relying on the probability that a salient of human nature could cause the gang to entrap itself. Admittedly, if the white raiders did do the opposite of what Kelly hoped, the least important half of the gang could be wiped out; but that was probably a specious argument, for one man could play many parts, and the activities of Vic Bales and his boys suggested that those involved were readily interchangeable in the roles of redman or white.

Down the rift they went, echoes packing where rock walls rose vertically. The piece of the trail which passed through the great crack was about two hundred yards long, but the floor was level throughout and the journey down it easy enough. Kelly emerged from the shadowy fissure to fifty yards of fairly open going before the beaten way became Renton's main street and he drew level with the first houses on either hand and saw that the painted villains were still doing all the damage they could ahead of him.

Caught completely off guard, the town had barely retaliated as yet. It was evident that the 'redmen' were extracting every advantage they could from the lack of return fire, and were also mocking the weak response. Kelly drew and cocked his revolver as he watched the badmen milling, then took aim and fired at the rider circling nearest to him. It was instantly a case of the surpriser surprised, for Kelly's bullet plucked the feather out of the badman's hair and caused him to gape round in startlement. Eyes filling with fright, he turned his head again and yelled in alarm to his comrades, his voice taking on a thick Irish-American brogue which could not be mistaken for other than a whiteman's accents.

Kelly went on spurring down the middle of the way. Again he fired over the narrowing gap between him and the enemy. Then he heard volley after volley begin ripping away from the guns of the ranch party. One of the fake Indians toppled from his saddle and curled up on the damp earth at the middle of the way, but the renegades were constantly on the move and no easy marks. They were also shooting back by this time — professional gunhands to a man — and there was a cry of pain from Brad Cullins, while a horse vented an agonized neigh and slumped onto its belly, bringing a bellow of dismay from 'Turkey' Bronson.

Immediately conscious of fire decreasing from his own side, Kelly craned swiftly to get a clear view of what had just happened, and he saw that Bronson's horse had dropped on the slant and promptly blocked off much of the street surface that was available to the charging cowboys. Phil Jordan, Trench, Dobbs and Arnie Grigson had been forced to heave back sharply to avoid the collapsed animal, and their mounts had instantly slithered round and bunched up, thus producing an element of chaos. Obviously encouraged by this sight, the fake redmen — who had been on the brink of flight — checked and screwed tightly round in their saddles, shooting with a more deliberate aim at their so abruptly incommoded attackers.

Kelly and the ranchmen with space before them had halted by now. They were attempting to cover their bumping comrades with some straighter shooting of their own. For several moments the fight became a far more static affair. A bullet flicked Kelly's right sleeve, and another rang against his left stirrup iron and sprang up to slightly nick his jaw. As a matter of prudence, he swung out of his saddle, realizing that he made a perfect target perched high and, using his horse for cover, blazed back at the man — his original target in fact — who had come so close to killing him, and he saw the other reel out of leather and lie still. But this success was no sooner registered than Arnie Grigson jerked upright in his seat, swore aloud, coughed blood and pitched off his horse, landing face down in the street and writhing feebly as a backing mount trampled all over him.

There was an urgent shouting from higher up the street. Kelly looked beyond the surviving badmen to where the voices were being raised. He saw townsmen emerging from the buildings at the further end of the main street. One of the figures wore a star on his chest and was directing those about him to take cover and begin shooting at the renegades. It looked as if the three painted individuals still dangerously active were about to be annihilated, but then the very thing that Kelly had hoped for occurred as a body of riders came galloping into town from the west with pistols flashing.

The townsmen exposed at the opposite end of the street spun to face the newcomers. Most of them, recognizing the odds, scurried back into the buildings from which they had issued at once, but a few held their ground and blasted a shot or two at the attacking badmen. Then one of these braver souls crumpled to the ground and started to thresh about in agony, a sight which caused his companions to lose their courage immediately and scuttle back into the buildings which their even less stout-hearted neighbours had fled into ahead of them.

Kelly scowled. What he had just witnessed at the other end of town struck him as rather poor, but he supposed that the sheriff and other men along there had only behaved as ninety nine men out of a hundred would have behaved in the face of gunfire and charging horses. Yet there was more to it than that, for a potential barrier had been removed, and the incoming villains now had a clear path down which to ride to the aid of the surviving 'redmen', who were still shooting it out with Kelly and the ranchmen.

Lifting his aim, Kelly prepared to throw a bullet among the riders pounding onwards up street of him, but the hammer of his gun snapped against a fired shell, warning him that his weapon was empty. Unsettled by the onset from the west, Kelly's horse skittered and sidled away from its master, exposing him fully to the fire triggered in his direction; so, deciding that it would be suicidal to attempt a reload standing in the open, he dived into an alley on his right and scampered towards its further end, spinning out the used contents of his Colt's cylinder as he went.

Coming to the lots, he sought shelter behind the corner of the fence on his left. Taking cartridges from a trouser-pocket, he thumbed the swiftest of reloads — all too aware through every second of the increasing ferocity of the battle noises from the street — and then resumed movement, passing down the lots until he came to the end of the next alley but one to the west of him. He entered this passageway, judging that it should stand even with the newly arrived badmen at its street exit, and pelted down its length, emerging opposite the now milling newcomers who were shooting fast and threatening to wipe out Sizeland and the Bar S cowboys fighting in his company.

At a total advantage for the moment, Kelly fired among the circling horsemen from almost pointblank range, cutting down two of them in short order. But now a man who sat tall in the saddle twigged Kelly's presence. The fellow twisted towards the alleyway, black-eyed and menacing, and he fired twice with a new Remington, the thunderclaps of sound seeming to merge into a single explosion, and Kelly heard the first slug go ricocheting off the wall behind him and felt the second put a tiny nick in his right ear, hot blood at once sprinkling his shoulder.

Crouching fast, his mouth shaping a wordless curse, Kelly shot upwards, and his bullet struck the dark-orbed villain in the throat and burst out of the other's nape, no doubt severing the badman's spine on the way, for the fellow came down like a rag doll and that was the end of him. It had been well done. Kelly knew it, and that he was capable of doing still better. So he jacked himself to the vertical once more and looked across the emptying street before him to where the short-necked, powerful figure of Vic Bales was now glowering at him in shocked amazement from his gelding's back. "Yeah, I'm still alive and kicking, you polecat!" he shouted.

Pudgy face craning, Bales moved up the street a yard or two on his restrained and now abruptly bucking horse, and the fleshy villain snapped off a quick shot at Kelly, missing by inches. The man would have done well to let his mount go on, but his miss had obviously filled him with fury. Teeth bared, he yanked brutally at his horse's mouth and tried to fetch it through an impossibly tight arc, clearly to bring his gun back into play immediately. The horse almost fell, but it was evidently a very strong one and, resisting its rider's abuse with all the power of its neck and haunches, came to a halt. Bales swore at it, rowelling with heels which struck harder and harder; then, wild-eyed and fearful — for his situation was plainly a parlous one — he attempted to make the best of a bad job, twisting right round in his saddle and shooting at Kelly as Kelly blazed at him.

Bales, overstretched, missed again, but Kelly's bullet pierced him beneath the right armpit and flung his torso to the front once more. This time he accepted the fact of what had occurred and released his mount's head from the awful pressure which he had been exerting upon the bit, and the brute gave its neck a violent shake and then lunged up the street, its long strides soon carrying it beyond Kelly's restricted view between walls.

It seemed the fight ought to have been over; but it wasn't. Guns still banged, though the firing soon petered a little and, kneeling forward to get a view of the street around the front corner of the building on his right, Kelly saw that four of the gangsters were still in their saddles and aiming their guns in a slightly confused and half-hearted manner at anybody or anything that moved to the east of them.

Then a clearer head among the villains urged flight, and the men wheeled their horses about and set off westwards — only to check within yards; for the townsmen had found strength in numbers during the preceding minute or two and were now blocking the upper end of the street in such force that the fugitives would be inviting almost certain death to approach them even at full gallop on horseback. "Better take it as read, boys!" Kelly shouted grimly to the badmen, shooting the hat off their nominal leader's head with such precision that they instantly dropped their weapons and lifted their hands.

Kelly stepped out into the street. He peered westwards, looking beyond the two ranks of townsmen who barred it about a hundred and fifty yards away. There was no sign of Vic Bales anywhere. He had neither been taken prisoner nor, to judge from the empty land to the west of Renton — which ought still to hold his presence if he had gone past before the folk up yonder had taken their stand — got clear and away. So where had the sidewinder got to? Kelly would stake his bottom dollar that the villain had received a bad wound — perhaps even a mortal one — and could not be far away; but he was given little time to consider it just then, for the man wearing the sheriff's star came running down the street and shouted: "It is you, Mr Sizeland! Are you in charge here?"

"No, Adey!" the master of the Bar S called back. "You see the man — Deputy United States Marshal Kelly!"

"Hello, Marshal!" Sheriff Adey greeted, passing the four prisoners — who were already covered by at least a dozen guns — and panting to a stop a few feet short of Kelly. "What's been happening here? I vow and declare, sir, I'm at a loss! There's a citizen lying dead near my office door. Judge Reed himself will require me to answer for the poor guy's death."

"I'll do the answering," Kelly said shortly. "I'm the judge's man."

"You're welcome, sir," Adey assured him, genuine relief showing on his square, rather goggle-eyed face, with its flattened nose and ribbons of wrinkled skin running down the insides of the cheeks. "If you like, we can talk in my office."

"Not today," Kelly replied, conscious of the persistent drizzle and the long evening's decreasing light. "You can lock up the prisoners, Sheriff, and I reckon Mr Sizeland can tell you most of what you wish to know. I've still got heaps to do before I can sign off for the night."

"Like what, Marshal?"

"Like putting salt on the tails of the two top varmints in this sorry yarn," Kelly answered. "One of them, Victor Bales, is still skulking around in your bailiwick. Didn't you see him come galloping your way a few minutes ago?"

Frowning, Adey shook his head.

"Heavy guy — ugly as sin?"

The sheriff shook his head again. "I could have been indoors, but nobody went past — going west."

"He must have turned off the

street," Kelly said irritably. "But can you believe nobody saw it?"

Adey raised his voice and asked the obvious question, but there was no answer from anybody on the scene.

"Seems not, Sheriff," Kelly acknowledged. "So did he turn off to the left or right? I fancy the left, since he was tight up on that side.

"I'll help you search, Marshal."

"Obliged," Kelly responded. "You might ask a man or two to search on the right."

"Okay," Adey said quiescently.

"But Bales is hurt, mind," Kelly warned, "and sure to be dangerous. So — careful!"

"Williams?" the sheriff wondered. "Askew?"

Nods came from two men standing nearby, rifles at the ready.

"Thanks," Adey said. "You heard the marshal just then. Careful, eh?" He gestured with his right hand. "Off you go, boys!"

Followed by Adey, Kelly crossed the

street, angling for the nearest of the alleys there. "You go to the right," he said, as they hurried through the narrow place. "I'll take the other direction."

"What's your reasoning for that?" the sheriff inquired, sounding a trifle exasperated.

"He could have doubled back this way," Kelly explained. "But he needn't have. It's just a matter of covering the most ground we can in the shortest time."

They came out on the lots. Here they parted, moving to either hand. Making another reload as he went, Kelly padded watchfully eastwards. He was aware of soaring rock on his right and all manner of fences and small buildings ahead of him. His senses strained, but there was no movement in the vicinity, and his surroundings, so drab and damp, hinted at more that was forlorn than menacing.

Pointing his gun, Kelly peered into the shadows and ill-scented corners about him, the tremors of urgency in his mind building to a compulsive throb, and he took issue with himself, for he realized that instinct had already told him what Vic Bales had done and that he was squandering time on his own doubts. Badly hurt, Bales would be seeking help, and he could only get that from one source. His goal now was almost certainly the home of Taylor Vaughan in South Hill. That meant, once out of sight of the men on the main street, he would indeed have doubled back and, using the lots, sought to regain the great fissure that carried the trail eastwards out of Renton. Yet, knowing this, Kelly still wanted some definite proof of it, and his search for the evidence went on until, arriving at the end of the lots — where an overhung path of sort squared round to join the street — he glimpsed fresh blood on a spray of new leaf that bowed down to about the height that a passing rider would brush against. Well, that blood, just turning sticky now, could only have come from one source; and, being this closely placed to the exit from town, it could likewise only mean that Bales had passed this way several minutes ago and managed to enter the climbing rift beyond town with the same kind of rapid stealth which had taken him off the main street without anybody noticing his sudden disappearance. Depending on his physical state — and the condition of his horse — he could already be miles out on the trail to South Hill and now impossible to catch short of Taylor Vaughan's home.

Again cursing himself and his own deliberate nature, Kelly jogged out to the street and then kept his trot going until he reached the spot — which was just beyond the ground where Rancher Sizeland and a well-dressed man who appeared to be a doctor were examining the casualties among the employees of the Bar S — where his horse had stopped after turning away from him during the gun battle with the renegades. He noticed that Abe Trench and Harry Dobbs were among the slightly wounded and paused to ask how things were with his earlier saviours. "Aw, wouldn't you know it?" foreman Brad Cullins observed disgustedly. "Those two couldn't even get themselves decently plugged! Trench shot himself in the toe, and Dobbs got his ass bitten by a scared dog. It's enough to make a man weep!"

Sharing a wink between the two shamefaced sufferers, Kelly mounted up; then, fetching his horse round, eased past the figures in the street, saying: "See you tomorrow, Mr Sizeland — all being well. I'm bound for South Hill."

"Good gracious, man!" the rancher called after him. "That's miles away!"

"I know," Kelly replied ruefully. "I'm damned if I know why the Good Lord put it there!"

Kelly trotted his horse to the edge of town, let it climb the ascent away from Renton at an easy pace, then drove it to a gallop across the high meadows beyond the rift. He soon came to the place where he and the men from the Bar S had earlier left the trail from the Ablett mine. Now he took full note of the beaten path which stretched eastwards from the junction and headed out over the dimming earth towards the not far distant plains. He kept watching for Vic Bales, quick or dead, every yard of the way; but, with the final departure of the light, the exercise grew futile, and he became glad enough just to watch but for himself and his mount, leaving the rest to a heavenly jurisdiction.

The ride went without mishap. Though Kelly's horse had been worked on the range earlier that day, it had clearly not been pushed until now, and it covered the miles with a free stride that seemed to take no account of night and the hazards of the country. In fact it wasn't a great deal more than an hour later when, topping a rise under a clearing sky, Kelly made out the lights of South Hill low in the darkness before him and was able to close upon the town with the certainty that he had exactly followed his route over the last fifteen miles.

Yet he had come this far only to face the much larger problems which remained. Most immediate of these was the fact that he must now find out where Taylor Vaughan lived. That done, he would then have to try approaching the address without encountering trouble; for, if the wounded Bales had made it to South Hill — and there was no good reason to suppose that he hadn't — the marshal's coming would be anticipated, since Kelly had made it abundantly plain to Bales that he was no ghost in the moment they had exchanged fire.

There was another thing — a subtlety, perhaps, but it couldn't be ignored. Asking around after Vaughan's address could prove dangerous of itself. In a town where the Union

Pacific employed a good number of people — and the manager had his contacts — word could be hurried to Vaughan about the lawman who was seeking his address, and that could give the manager an additional edge in preparing a counter stroke; so all things considered, he thought it might prove wiser to pay Judge Harrison Reed a quick visit and pick up the information he required there. Thus he would avoid talking to any source but the one that presently knew most about his affairs. There had also been that suggestion this morning that the judge might invite Taylor Vaughan in again for the evening, so there was the possibility that he would find the manager at dinner on Second Street. This could mean that he would carry an element of danger into the Reed household — which he didn't want to do, if only because Jean Troy was there — but, with the renegades now either dead or under lock and key, he felt that it would be sensible to take

Vaughan into custody before the man could either chance making a break for it or calling in legal aid that might make holding him hard to achieve. All this, of course, quite obviously subject to the flux of circumstances.

Kelly slowed his horse into town. South Hill was lighted with flares, but these had been sparingly placed, and the streets were patchily illuminated because of it. There was, however, light enough to ride by safely, and it was only as he entered Second Street and neared the judge's house that Kelly found himself in an unlighted district. With his mount's progress now reduced to walking pace, he peered intently through the gloom before him, seeking details half remembered from his earlier visit to the Reed property, and he was nearing the judge's front gate, when he glimpsed movement in the night ahead and then dimly made out the shapes of a horse and a clumsily fashioned man standing near its head.

Reining to a halt, Kelly sensed the

other peering at him hard and, realizing that he was placed against a faint glow of light from the nearby main street, lowered his right hand to the butt of his revolver. Fearing that this was something which must be faced, Kelly hunched forward a little and asked conversationally: "That you, Bales?"

10

KELLY heard a sharp intake of breath, then the hiss of steel against leather as a pistol was whipped out of its holster. Fire streaked at him, its reflection glimmering on the black figure behind the gun, and he felt the bullet clip the left side of his gunbelt, gouging deep enough to burn and stink. Drawing fast, Kelly blazed a return, shots pulsing back and forth after that for two seconds more, and the man standing beside the now prancing horse suddenly flopped down on his belly and lay motionless.

Dismounting, Kelly cocked his weapon anew, making the most he could of the metallic noise, then closed slowly and deliberately on the downed figure — crouching abruptly and thrusting the muzzle of his Colt against his victim's head. Nothing happened, and Kelly prodded a couple of times, knowing how painful a conscious man would have found such treatment, but there was still no reaction and, pretty sure that his enemy had gone home, he thrust a boot under the man's body and tipped him onto his back, a face that was undoubtedly Vic Bales's just visible to his newly adjusted sight in the faint glow that paled towards him from the main street.

Putting out his left hand, Kelly felt for a throat pulse, but there was nothing there and he accepted that Bales was dead. Then, hearing footfalls on the nearby garden path, he straightened up and gazed towards the sounds, conscious immediately of the beam from a bull's-eye lantern moving over the paving stones and approaching the judge's front gate from the direction of the house. Moments later, a just visible figure arrived at the entrance to the property and the ray of light was tilted towards Kelly's presence. "What's happened out here?"

Judge Harrison Reed's voice demanded authoritatively. "I heard shots being fired!"

"It's me, Judge — Sam Kelly," the survivor of the gunfight answered. "I've just finished a job I only half did over in Renton."

"Kelly, eh?" the judge said stiffly. "Who's that man lying there?"

"Victor Bales," Kelly replied. "I told you about him this morning. I guess you'd call him the field leader of those renegades who have been creating so much havoc about."

"I see. And you're from Renton now?"

"Yes, sir. We put paid to the gang over there earlier this evening."

"Did you indeed!" Judge Reed observed, sounding faintly jolted. "So quickly!"

"I guess I had the luck, sir," Kelly said as honestly as he could, "and they made the mistakes. I need Taylor Vaughan now — and it's done with."

"Taylor Vaughan is in my house at

this moment, Kelly."

"I sort of half hoped he might be — recalling what you said before we parted this morning."

"Well, yes," Harrison Reed said uncertainly. "I have, er, done nothing towards restraining him."

"He's there," Kelly said — "that's what matters. I didn't see how you could do a lot to help, with things as they stood. Hard evidence was needed, but Vaughan's arrest should stand now. There ought to be witnesses enough against him back in Renton."

"I see."

"You're the legal authority here, Judge," Kelly reminded, surprised that the other seemed so wooden.

"Indeed," the judge snapped, suddenly crisp again. "Come in, please, and let's get on with it."

"Bales?"

"He's dead, isn't he?"

"Yes, sir."

"Then leave him lying there, confound it!" Harrison Reed advised sharply.

"What the devil else can you do for a dead man?"

"Get him off the street," Kelly suggested, shrugging to himself as he walked over to the judge's gate."

"Follow me," the other ordered, facing about and striding back towards the house, the thin beam of his lantern jiggling from side to side ahead of him.

Kelly walked after the man, swiftly reloading some of his Colt's fired chambers as he went, and he entered the judge's well-lighted hall with his weapon once more cocked and ready.

They went through to the room with the white fireplace and in which so much else was white, and Kelly saw Taylor Vaughan sitting comfortably in an armchair before him, brandy glass in one hand and a fragrant cigar in the other. The U.P. manager appeared completely at his ease and looked Kelly up and down with a superior eye that contained no trace of either surprise or fear. Indeed he showed a faint amusement as he took in the marshal's damp figure and the rain-dulled badge upon his chest. "Good evening," he said with an exaggerated politeness. "I see it isn't only cats that fall upon their feet."

"How's that again?" Kelly asked, openly covering the manager with his Colt.

"I see you've become the law," Taylor Vaughan explained, "in its public manifestation. You were a down-and-out in my office yesterday, were you not?"

"Cut it out, mister!" Kelly warned. "Sass is sass at any level, and so's a dirty crook! I'll be a happy man the day they lock you away for forty years!"

"Spits, too, doesn't he, sir?" Vaughan observed, glancing humorously to where the judge had just extinguished the bull's-eye lantern and was wrinkling a nostril at the stink of its fumes. "What's this all about, Kelly?"

"You know good-and-well what it's all about!" Kelly retorted. "I suppose we're going to have one of those scenes in which everything has to be spelled out. Very well then! You've been the man behind a pack of raiders, Vaughan, and filling a heck of a lot more than the pockets of your pants. I'd like to tell your story in the lodge of Sitting Bull, then leave you to the attentions of him and his people. I figure that's the way you'd get what you most richly deserve. I reckon those redskins would split you in two with wild horses!"

"You live with some ugly thoughts — Marshal," the manager sneered. "Big talk — but how much of it can you prove?"

"With the help of some good and able folk," Kelly replied, "I smashed your gang over in Renton this evening. Vic Bales is lying dead in the street outside, but we've prisoners enough to confirm my story in court. I've got you dead-to-rights, Vaughan, and all the educated wriggling and smart talk in the world won't help you now. Savvy?"

Taylor Vaughan yawned, again looking at the judge amusedly. "A strange order of bedtime story, Harrison. By God, yes! But it's his triumph and self-righteousness that offend me most. He reminds one of a braying ass, does he not?"

Kelly stiffened. He had expected further mockery from Taylor Vaughan, but the manager was now just too confident in his behaviour and, sickened by the unthinkable conclusion which he suddenly realized must be the truth, he glanced quickly towards the judge and saw that he was covered by a twin-barrelled derringer. "Lower the hammer of your revolver, Kelly," Harrison Reed ordered, "take the weapon to the mantelpiece, place it there, then retreat to your present position."

Feeling utterly betrayed, Kelly obeyed the judge's instructions to the letter, then he drew himself up and said: "It's a law of Nature and the sad truth sure enough — the scum comes to the top!"

Rising up, big, powerful, and infuriated, Taylor Vaughan let fly with a punch straight from his right shoulder. The blow burst like a bombshell on the point of Kelly's jaw and sent him staggering backwards into contact with the edge of the hall door, which stood open into the room. Bouncing off the woodwork, Kelly fell upon his back and lay in a dazed state, while the violently swinging door struck the wall behind it and vibrated noisily there. Vaughan stalked towards his victim, obviously prepared to do serious damage to the supine figure with the toe of his boot, but Harrison Reed threw up a staying hand and said sharply: "Stop it, Taylor — that's enough!"

"Why?" Taylor Vaughan hissed.

"Because I say so," the judge snapped. "I don't want him bleeding all over my parlour."

The Union Pacific manager seemed to find this a weak excuse, and Kelly — who had by this time recovered enough to receive a clear picture of the man above him — watched Taylor Vaughan shut his eyes and fight for self-control, only just achieving it. After that the manager backed off and said: "Harrison, we have no choice but to kill him. You must see that at least as well as I."

"I know it full well," the judge acknowledged tersely. "We'll take him down into the cellar. You can blow out his brains in there."

"But the noise of the shot!" Vaughan protested. "You keep staff in your house, sir. The women will hear the gun go off!"

"The women are already upstairs and asleep at the back of the house," Harrison Reed said. "The sound of the shot won't reach them from the cellar, and you'll be able to extract the body through the fanlight and then carry it away from the side of the house."

"All the dirty work seems to be mine," Vaughan remarked bitterly.

"Like rank, my boy," the judge said cynically, "age hath its privileges."

Kelly climbed slowly to his feet, scowling at Harrison Reed. "Why?" he demanded. "Aren't you a big enough man already?"

"Neither big enough nor rich enough," Judge Reed confessed. "Given ability — with which I am sufficiently gifted — ninety per cent of a man's ambitions depend on money. The road to Washington has to be paved with gold coin."

"All good things depend on money," Taylor Vaughan reflected. "There's a measure of luck involved too. You seem to have more than your share of that, Kelly."

"Indeed," the judge agreed, his face screwing up as if his mouth were full of lemon juice. "It was intended that you should die on the way to Renton."

"I nearly did," Kelly said. "Your men tried hard enough. But perhaps you're right about that luck."

"If so," Vaughan commented, "you've used it all up now."

"You mentioned a cat not so long

ago," Kelly recalled. "Don't cats have nine lives?"

"Not when they receive a bullet through the brain," the judge informed him grimly. "Let's do this thing, Taylor. The nights at this time of the year are not so long."

"Lead us to your cellar then," Vaughan said, picking up Kelly's revolver from the mantelpiece.

Nodding, the judge headed for the way out of the room, gesturing at the same time for his accomplice to bring the captive along, and the three of them were about to step out into the hall, when Jean Troy entered, forcing them back with the shotgun which she pressed against Harrison Reed's breastbone. "Oh, no, you don't, Judge!" she cautioned. "Throw that little gun into the corner! I've been listening out here, and I've heard every wicked word you've spoken!"

"You surely timed it just right, Jean!" Kelly declared fervently, wresting his Colt from the hand of Taylor Vaughan.

"I reckoned I was as good as dead!"

"The housekeeper and I heard the shooting outside," the girl explained rather breathlessly. "Then I heard your voice downstairs. I knew something was wrong — so I threw on my clothes and crept down here. The shotgun I took from the judge's study."

"Good girl!" Kelly approved. "You truly use what you've got in your head! Well, it's total disgrace for His Honour and a felon's lot for Taylor Vaughan. Everything is in the open now — and I can add you to my list of witnesses." He forced the two glowering crooks well back into the parlour. "Would you like to add to the help you've given, Jean?"

"Anything, Sam."

"Then go and root out the sheriff," Kelly instructed. "Tell him I need help to get these characters behind bars. It'd be too risky to take them out into the night by myself. A couple of riled up copperheads would be far safer to handle!"

"Right away," the girl said.

"You'd better put that shotgun back where you found it," Kelly urged. "You might frighten the sheriff to death if you dragged that along to him."

Jean nodded, smiling faintly, and was about to make her way into the hall, when a lumpy figure — brow red with gore, eyes cloudy, and obviously at his life's extremity — shuffled onto the threshold of the room and stopped there, pistol levelled. — He appeared to have just enough strength and clarity of wit left to shape the thin twist of his bloodless lips into the words: "Get 'em up!"

For that moment Kelly was frankly amazed and, bereft because of it, stood numb while Taylor Vaughan reclaimed the Colt that he had taken from the other not a minute before. How much killing did Vic Bales require? Yet he could see what had happened. The bullet which had flattened Bales had no more than clipped the man's crown and rendered him unconscious for a short while. The fellow was still dying of that first wound which he had received in Renton. It looked as if he had lasted just long enough to come in here and turn things for the forces of evil that were still so strongly present. This could now be the end for both Sam Kelly and Jean Troy. It was the most crushing luck!

"Went to — to your place," Bales muttered at Taylor Vaughan. "Your man said — said you were — were over here."

"The judge and I had much to talk about," the U.P. manager responded, watching Bales intently, for it was plain that the man was not going to hold up much longer.

Then it happened suddenly. Bales dropped into a heap, his revolver exploding as his legs buckled, and Judge Reed — who had been heading for the spot where his derringer lay — let out a cry of pain and grabbed the back of his right leg, sprawling forward onto the floor an instant later.

It was again Kelly's turn to react speedily. He swung over his right fist and struck Taylor Vaughan on the left side of his jaw. The manager went reeling across the room, struck the corner of the mantelpiece, and then folded to the floor, coming to rest in a sitting position in the angle formed by the boards and the wall itself. Dazed, but not so badly that he didn't know what was happening, he considered Kelly for a moment; then, still in possession of his weapon, he upped the Colt and covered the man who had just hit him, clearly getting ready to put a bullet into his enemy; but Jean Troy — who was still holding her shotgun, if with the muzzles pointed at the floor — quickly jerked the twin barrels level and pressed both triggers at once. The noise was thunderous, and fire and black smoke belched, the big weapon's recoil almost tearing it out of the girl's grasp; then, as the fumes pulsed into chaplets, Kelly looked through the hovering rings and saw that his foe had been blasted into a human ruin and must have died instantly.

Then a lighter gunshot cracked out. Kelly felt the wind of a bullet blow on the bridge of his nose. He screwed his head to the left, seeing what he had expected to see; for the accidentally wounded Harrison Reed had contrived to reach his derringer, rolled into a sitting position with the weapon raised, and just fired that very near miss at the man whom he had made a marshal. But the derringer still had that second barrel, and one forty-four calibre slug fired at short range was quite sufficient to tear the life out of the average man.

With a start of horror — and his nape prickling — Kelly leapt away from the judge's immediate aim and landed beside the revolver which had lately spilled from the dead Taylor Vaughan's nerveless grasp. Crouching, Kelly got a grip on the Colt and screwed towards Harrison Reed, settling on his heels.

Their eyes met across the room. Kelly thumbed off a shot, more to unsettle his man than in the expectation of scoring a hit; but his bullet went home, rocking the judge; and he rose up then, chopping at the hammer with the edge of his left hand. He got off three more shots in the space of a moment, and the lead swept Harrison Reed flat and left him lying inert.

Lowering his revolver, Kelly let its barrel hang down the side of his leg. After that he walked slowly across the room to where the judge lay. Harrison Reed had been shot twice through the heart and was unquestionably dead. Kelly considered the corpse for a moment or two, then unpinned the badge from his chest and threw it down beside the deceased. The judge had been a most superior man — a real power in the Wyoming Territory — but his brains had made a fool of him in the end. For he had appointed the wrong man marshal and thereby worked his own undoing.

Walking back to where Jean Troy stood gazing at him pensively, Kelly put his left hand on her right shoulder and said: "We'd better go and see the sheriff. Explaining this shambles to him won't be easy."

"Sam, I can't believe any of it," the girl said, clapping a palm to her forehead. "Yet somehow I know it had to be."

"I reckon it's me for the quiet life after this," Kelly said.

"Doing what?" Jean scorned.

Kelly bowed his head until it touched hers. "If we put our heads together — like this — I believe we can figure out something, don't you? How about a joint adventure — of this kind or that?"

Jean smiled. "I'll think about it."

Kelly hoped she might — and knew she would.

Other titles in the Linford Western Library:

TOP HAND
Wade Everett

The Broken T was big. But no ranch is big enough to let a man hide from himself.

GUN WOLVES OF LOBO BASIN
Lee Floren

The Feud was a blood debt. When Smoke Talbot found the outlaws who gunned down his folks he aimed to nail their hide to the barn door.

SHOTGUN SHARKEY
Marshall Grover

The westbound coach carrying the indomitable Larry and Stretch headed for a shooting showdown.